Lock Down Publications and Ca$h
Presents

I0664139

DRILL
CITY

Written By
ZAY'TOWVEN

First Edition 2025

Printed in the United States of America

This is a work of fiction. Names, characters, places, and incidents either are products of the author's imagination or are used fictitiously. Any similarity to actual events or locales or persons, living or dead, is entirely coincidental.

Lock Down Publications
P.O. Box 944
Stockbridge, GA 30281
www.lockdownpublications.com

Like our page on Facebook: Lock Down Publications
www.facebook.com/lockdownpublications.ldp

Stay Connected with Us!

Text **LOCKDOWN** to 22828 to stay up-to-date with new releases, sneak peaks, contests and more…

Like our page on Facebook:
Lock Down Publications

Join Lock Down Publications/The New Era Reading Group

Visit our website:
www.lockdownpublications.com

Follow us on Instagram:
Lock Down Publications

Email Us: We want to hear from you!

Chapter 1

(ZARO)

8 a.m. Rockford IL

"Why the fuck are we sitting here again?" Telay asked.

I looked at him, disappointed. That he would ask a dumb question like that was beyond me. "Did you forget everything we discussed?" I replied with sarcasm.

Telay and I had been friends since as long as I could remember, and no matter how stupid he came off, I trusted him with my life. He wasn't a rat in any shape or form, and that counted for everything. It's the reason we were sitting here in the first place.

Lawndale Bank, that was the target. My plan was to set up surveillance and find out who was responsible for opening and closing the establishment. This bit of info would be the key component to successfully pulling off this heist. I kept my eyes trained on the front door when suddenly, a white BMW turned into one of the parking slots. A tall, slender white guy jumped out of the car, swinging a briefcase. I perked up in my seat, "I think that's our boy."

"Let's hope so, because I'm ready to get out of here. It's too early to be sitting in an empty parking lot," Telay complained.

I paid close attention to his movements and took special note of the Per-Mar security guarding him inside. I slide the car into gear and eased out of the parking slot. "A'ight, I've seen enough," I stated.

4

"When you gonna do this bank thing?" Telay asked.

I chuckled. "What's so funny?" he asked again.

"Oh, you didn't know? Just like in Paris, when I say 'we', I mean we . . . are definitely gunna rob this bank." I chuckled between sentences. "I got to go over the plan with everybody, then we'll go from there."

Telay looked surprised, "Wait a minute, you mean everybody like Comboy and Bang?"

"Of course. Did you think I was going to do this on my own?" I replied.

"Well, kind of."

"What, you scared or somethin'?" I joked. I'd known Telay for a long time; his heart was strong, and I knew he'd know I was joking with the scared remark.

"I'm with you regardless, fam. You know you my day one."

"I'm glad to hear that, because I got some shit planned that could take us to the next level. This bank is only the stepping stone to lock this city down. It's our turn, T," I assured him.

Telay nodded, "Whatever you need, fam, just let me know. I'm going all the way with you."

"That's good to know. Call Cowboy and ask his location. The quicker we can put this play into action, the better."

Telay dialed Cowboy's number, talked briefly, then ended the call and looked over to me. "He in Waaco at his sister crib."

I let out a sigh and shook my head. "I hate going out there."

Waaco consists of grouped-together project buildings on the west end of town. Its name, an acronym for 'We Assassinate All Cowardly Organizations,' was infamous. I's inhabitants are a mixture of Gangster Disciples, Vice Lords, and some new breeds, all working in sync with one another. They forged a reputation for being savage, and cut-throat renegades. Their loyalty didn't lie with their respective mobs, though; it lay with the commitment they had to each other from years of eating off the same plate. They considered themselves a family, and that's what made them infamous in the city. Their dope line ran 24 hours a day, and they served only the best product. The complex was gated, making it one way through, and the lanes in and out worked immensely to their advantage. They didn't allow any outsiders. The only people welcomed in were potential shoppers.

Waaco had the best heroin in the city. People came from all over to cop what they had. Flex and Remo sat at the helm of its lucrative empire, with Lil' Mick as their top shooter. They called themselves the Wolf Pack, and they protected their empire efficiently. Lil' Mick was a young, cold-hearted, dangerous person, with more bodies on him than a serial killer. Needless to say, if you found yourself staring down a barrel, he was the last person you'd want holding the gun.

Savon, Cowboy's sister, had been a resident of Waaco for 7 years; she moved there right before Cowboy went to prison. Cowboy hated living there; it was like living in a caged zoo with Flex and Remo as the zookeepers. It's hard for the rest of the city to imagine a group of project buildings being owned by two black men, so they buried their identities in the mountain of legal paperwork that confirmed the purchase of said land from the city. Because of this, the low-income government assistance programs were no more; that didn't stop Flex and Remo from making the rent affordable though. It was their enterprise, and they ran it with an iron fist.

"Enter the dragon, the muthafuckin' dragon," I uttered as I pulled into the gates of hell. Savon lived in the last building towards the back of the complex. I drove with ease, trying not to arouse suspicion or any unwanted attention from the soldiers standing around. They watched me carefully as I rolled through. Lil' Mick had an itchy trigger finger, and he and I despised each other. I wanted to see him in a coffin more than anything in this world, but I'm a patient person and would soon have my chance to make him pay for the past. He stood about 5'9" or 10" with dreads, and was 130 pounds soaking wet. His debt with me is due to paid in what the Muslims call blood money. Revenge is a dish best served cold.

He stood out front of the building shooting dice with a few other Waaco goons as we pulled into the complex. "He's a bitch.", I said as I slid the car into park.

"Fuck him, fam," Telay assured me, trying to ease the tension I had broiling inside. Lil' Mick and I's beef originated from past damages left un-repaired, and him being a cocky, arrogant little prick while rubbing shit in my face whenever we got the chance was the base of it now. Whenever I would come around, he always wanted to crack jokes like I was some little broke, orphan-type kid. Mick wanted everybody to worship the ground he walked on, and refused to be one of his flunkies. Of the crowd of young men shooting dice, Mick was in the middle of the whole thing, instigating as he usually did.

"My point, 5," Mick clacked the dice and shouted as we stepped out of the car and approached the building. Telay trailed behind me as I tried to avoid Lil' Mick, but I knew interaction was inevitable.

"Zaro, you go to school today or what?" he said. I couldn't believe this nigga was trying to shoot the shit as if I fucked with him or something.

"Did you go?" I retorted with rivaling levels of sarcasm.

"Nigga, you betta watch your mouth when you talkin' to grown folks," Mick poured on. I hoped this would not be the straw that broke the camel's back and tried to keep my cool. I knew he didn't mean any real harm by his comments, but sometimes it was hard to decipher his level of sarcasm.

"Mick, you need to find someone to play with," I said to defuse the tension between us, but I was really in my chest about the matter.

"Chill out, nigga, I'm just shooting the shit at you," Mick said as Flex rolled up in his Audi A8. I felt somewhat relieved.

"Yeah, get over to your boss, shorty," I said with a smile. He trotted off to see what Flex wanted, while Telay and I brushed past the rest of the Waaco goons.

"Man, I thought he was gon' try some stupid shit, and we would've had to jump his dumb ass," Telay stated to me.

"He's not that dumb."

Cowboy's sister, Savon, lived on the 3rd floor. I tapped on the door, and Savon answered, looking sexy as ever. I've had a crush on her since I was a small kid; she wasn't that much older than me, but she was like a big sister to us all, not just to Cowboy.

"What's up, Zaro? Ya boy's in the back," she answered.

"Is that Nicole in there?" Telay asked, as he walked past the living room. "What's up, shorty?" Telay stretched his neck to get a good look at her. She just waved him off like she was a 'bad bitch' or something. Nicole was dark-skinned with a fat ass and had run through the whole projects. I didn't understand what Telay saw in her, but he liked them raunchy.

Cowboy's door was slightly ajar, and as we walked inside, we immediately noticed the smell—it reeked of marijuana.

"What's good with y'all?" he asked and slapped our hands. Bang, his right-hand man, was seated on the bean bag chair sacking up some nickel bags.

"You got that shit for sale?" Telay inquired with enticing eyes.

Bang nodded his head up and down; he wasn't one for talking much. He and Cowboy met in juvie and were thick as thieves. Cowboy said he had to save him from some Latin Kings while inside, and that's how they became friends. Cowboy did most of the talking for him, as he wasn't really a street guy. He attended private schools and lived in a two-parent household, unlike the rest of us. He frequently ran away when he was younger and now lived with his mentor, Cowboy, and Cowboy's sister.

"You wanted to talk about something?" Cowboy asked eagerly. He was a smooth, fast talker, and some would say he had a chip on his shoulder in an arrogant, egotistical type of way. While he may be perceived as a narcissist, to us he was a loyal friend and rider. He would bust his gun quick, though, and served time for killing his mother's boyfriend with a .22 revolver, which is how he got the name Cowboy to begin with. He served four years in Illinois Youth Center.

"I copped an ounce from that nigga PT," Bang replied.

Telay eyed the sacks hungrily and dug into his pocket. "Let me get one."

"So what you wanted to talk about?" Cowboy asked.

I took a seat on the bed. "I got a lick for us to hit."

"What you talkin' 'bout and how much in it?" he replied.

"Lawndale Bank. That mu'fuka got 200K inside of its vault every day, and I know how to get to it clean."

"Lil' Rodney Nemm got 45 years for robbing a bank just last week. That shit's risky," Bang interjected.

"Them niggas was dumb for bodyin' the security, for one, and for two, that shit was poorly coordinated. I want to kidnap the manager. He holds the keys to a piggy safe. I wanna hold his family hostage and make him rob the muthafucka himself," I explained. I looked to each one of them for a response.

Cowboy is usually the first to speak. "I'm not gonna front, that idea sounds great."

Next to speak was Telay. "What happens afterwards? Are we robbing banks for a living? I'm asking because you told me some other shit in the car, so what's to that?"

I looked at him with a glimmer. "I'm glad you're finally paying attention to something I said. I got some shit I'm working on with them IRA mu'fukas, and I wanna pull up on Kamar to see about a connect."

"What them IRA boys got to do with us? Last I checked, they wasn't fucking with the blacks on nothin'," Cowboy retorted.

"Shit, they got the connect on the guns we need to rob the bank, plus help us set up shop in the city," I explained. "My pops used to deal with them, and I talked to O'Riley a few weeks ago. He said if I need anything, to holla, so Imma call in a favor too."

"That don't mean he gone give you a load of guns to potentially use on him though," Cowboy replied.

"Don't worry. That white boy is greedy, he gone want that money, my boy," I reassured him.

"You got that all out of one conversation in passing?" Cowboy prodded.

I looked down at my phone and checked the time. "As a matter of fact, I got to meet them right now. You got any more questions?"

"You want to use the money from the bank to buy drugs and put us ahead in the streets," Telay stated.

"It's the easiest way to spend the money, as most people get caught by lavish spending." I looked around the room. "So what's the deal, y'all in or out?"

"You know I like money," Cowboy said. "What about you, Bang? You wit' us?"

"I'm wit' whatever, fam," Bang finally said.

"A'ight, Imma holler at the IRA, and we gone set this shit in motion."

The IRA were into human trafficking and gun running. They beefed with the Italians but didn't want a war with the blacks, so they kept their distance. They thought of blacks as a bunch of hyenas, but my father had a special bond with them. He'd dealt with them secretively, to what extent I don't know, but I remember O'Riley coming to my home often.

As I drove to the *Lucky 7* bar, O'Riley's hangout, I couldn't help but think the true reason I wanted to rob this particular bank was that it would affect Flex, and I hated the nigga. Waaco was in my direct line of sight, but I needed guns, drugs, and an army to make this thing work. I had no source of income to provide my men, so this meeting was extremely important; it could be a huge step in the right direction toward my ultimate goal. Lucky 7 was on the corner of 7th Street and Broadway. The strip was usually busy, especially with prostitutes, but the day was still early, making it appear deserted. The night brought a more lively party scene, however, and the Irish were known for turning it into a Las Vegas blade.

7th Street and Broadway was a prime spot for their line of work.

I parked on the gravel next to the pub and shook my head at how cheap they were with the parking lot, considering all the money they made. I hopped out the car and pulled my hoodie over my head, shielding me from the frosty winds. I walked toward the door with confidence—things were going to work out in my favor. A slight doubt slid into the back of my mind though, and I muttered, "I hope these crackers will fuck with me," as I got to the door. As I stepped inside, I noticed the bar was completely empty; I thought it odd considering the parking lot had a decent amount of cars in it. The bartender stood at the TV watching a UFC fight from the night before. He never switched his gaze as I took up a barstool, but as soon as I asked, "Is O'Riley here?" he turned his head sharply in my direction.

"Who's asking?" he demanded while looking me up and down, as if sizing me up.

"Zaro. He knows I'm coming.", I replied. He picked up the phone, said a few words, then ended the call.

"Sit tight. Marty will be up momentarily. Have a drink while you wait?"

"No, thanks."

"Suit yourself," he replied and went back to watching the fight on TV.

Marty was a heavyset guy with bright orange/red hair, and I thought he mimic'd the stereo-typical Irishman as he stood in the doorway. "Hey, Zaro, I'm glad you made it, mate."

"Thanks for inviting me," I said with a wide respectful grin. He led the way through the kitchen to a steel door. I gawked at the place, it was a lot bigger than it looked from the outside. The doorway led to a flight of stairs, and I stood at the top, almost frozen. The damp frigid air coming up from the bottom gave me an eerie feeling, and Marty must have seen the skepticism on my face because he told me, "O'Riley is waiting on you."

The basement was a whole other business; patrons were playing poker, watching strippers dance on poles, and engaging in drugs and prostitution. The men looked as though they'd been there for days with no sleep. This place was not as empty as it seemed on the surface because O'Riley ran an illegal gambling spot on top of prostitution. As I noticed a velvet room in the back, I saw O'Riley seated on a velvet booth wearing a Kangol hat with the button front. His beard was bushy; it gave him a biker look, and the eye patch added to that to give him a sinister, and somewhat cynical vibe. "Zaro, what brings you to the southside with us?"

"Business," I answered.

"I'm always up for that. How's your father?"

"He's doing time."

"That's fair. Now that we've engaged in pleasantries, what can I do for you, mate?"

I cleared my throat nervously; this was the moment of truth. He could either make or break me from here on out and there was no turning back. "I come to you with a business proposal. I'm hungry out here, and a few of my guys want to set up shop on the west side. I got this job planned out for a large sum of cash, but I need some stuff to aid in this mission."

"You sure you want to eat with a bunch of wolves? Thing is, this game isn't for everybody. I'm not sure what you think I can help you with, but I wouldn't mind knowing that you got up your sleeve," O'Riley asked curiously.

"I heard through the streets that you got a shipment of guns off that freight in Chicago, and I need some fronted. I can come up with the money shortly afterwards though, as it's a play for 200 grand," I explained.

"That sounds intriguing, but it don't seem real," O'Riley countered. "It sounds too good to be true."

I feel like everything is on the line right now so I pull out all the stops with my next statement, "I came to you because you did good business with my dad, and I want to tie up some loose ends of his. My father is doing a life bid right now, and seeing that he's taking his time to the tomb with him, I figured that would hold a little weight with you."

"That holds a lot with me, but you must know that everything that glitters isn't gold. Guns are a rare commodity out here, and these same guns you're asking for could get turned on me," he explained.

"That's not the case here. I'm on a mission that I'm sure you would want to be a part of," I said with professionalism.

"How so? I got the southside and Flex has the west. He won't let you or me infringe on his business. Plus, you ain't nothin' but a youngin', these niggas out here are savages." O'Riley spelled it out harshly.

"With all due respect, I don't fuck with Flex, and his days are numbered. If you give me the firepower. I know a lot more than what people expect of me.", I retorted with confidence. Must've been the right shit to say, 'cause that smirk on Oriley's face said he was interested in the potential opportunity.

"What you gon' do for a connect? How many soldiers you got? But the real shit is, you ain't got no cash to pay me if shit goes sideways. If you die, I'm outta my bread, and on top of that, if I hand you these guns, I'm in the mix with your war on Waaco," O'Riley implied.

"I swear, I'll keep you outta this, and the money will be in your hands in a few days. No cap." But as I finished explaining, I heard him scoff.

He glanced at Marty. "What you think, Marty?" he asked. Marty shrugged. O'Riley continued, "You'll have to let me think on this for a while. You want me to strike a match to some gasoline right now. This thing could blow up in your face and get us both involved in some shit neither of us can handle . . . I know exactly what you need though, and it's gonna run 20 grand. That's ONLY if I decide to get on board." He stood up and offered his hand, which meant the meet was over. We shook hands, and as I exited the door, I had mixed thoughts. I wondered if I'd actually accomplished what I set out to do.

Chapter 2

(O'RILEY)

As I eyed Zaro's back when he exited the game room, Marty asked me, "What you thinkin' about?"

"Does the apple fall far from the tree?" I pondered. "His father was a good man, and it was a shame how things went down with him, but we have to play this thing to our advantage. This may be the opportunity we've been waiting for on the westside. A window may come open for us if we let them niggas take each other out, but this little stunt might also bring Kamar out of hiding too," I said, while concocting a selfish plan to discard Zaro once his usefulness expires.

Kamar was the supplier for the westside, but since his clientele was exclusively his own people, everyone else had to cop from other sources. The current word was that Kamar was out the game, but I knew that to be a lie. Flex kept Waaco supplied with the best drugs, and both he and Kamar worked together back in the day. Zamad was with them strong, and I thought it would be beneficial for me to deal with his son and see what Zaro could bring to the table. Zamad was one of the connections I had needed to get some of that dope they had in them projects. I wanted to keep up with the westside, but Flex was a selfish, cutthroat muthafuka. I had to find another way back then. My take with Zamad was purely business, and if it weren't for me, he never would've met his whore of a baby mama. I sat back, thinking of all the ways this half-breed could be good to me, and unlike his father, I would have no qualms with tossing him aside like a crumpled piece of paper. The westside is going to be mine.

(ZARO)

I pulled up to MARS Car Mart, owned by an ex-drug lord my dad used to run with, figuring I could probably find some work his way. Judging by all the extravagant cars in the lot, I knew I was in the right place. I tipped my hat when I peeped a Lamborghini out front, but when my eyes eventually landed on a Maybach and BMW truck parked back-to-back, I realized they had to be the owners. "Oh shit!" I muttered.

Kamar was supposed to be out the game, but I knew that shit was a lie. That gut feeling is what brought me here today.

Kamar was the missing link I needed to take Flex out of Waaco. The Irish bring the guns, Kamar got the dope, and I'm the one holding this shit together. Kamar was smart, streetwise—if you know how to use that, it can get you far. He'd put a lot of people on back in the day, now it's my turn. I definitely wasn't trying to hear any of that 'out the game' shit either, as far as I was concerned, he owed me for my dad taking a life bid on his behalf. As I walked to the door, I couldn't help but take in my surroundings and all the beautiful cars. I even paused to imagine myself behind the wheel of a Porsche truck when a young white kid surprised me from behind.

"Can I help with something?" he asked.

I spun around, startled, as he continued, "I'm sorry, my name is Chris Wiggins."

"It's all good, Chris, I'm here to talk to Kamar," I said while fighting off my embarrassment for window shopping. He slick checked me up and down as I mentioned Kamar, and lo and behold, Kamar stepped outside, dappered down in a Tom Ford suit, like he was in a GQ magazine. I admired his swagger, though—it was different and not what I was accustomed to. He carried himself like a James Bond type, unlike the kingpin swagger I was used to seeing. Kamar walked with the confidence of a CEO, as if the world bowed before him with each step.

"What brings the god's son to my car lot today? I haven't seen you since you were just a little one. How is your Aunt?"

"I was just in the neighborhood," I answered while internally impressed I hadn't had to jog his memory about who I was.

"It's okay, I got it from here, Chris. Come to my office and let's talk, Zaro," he said while ushering for me to follow.

Kamar's office was an African safari museum—he had art all over the walls and crude weapons like spears on display. Needless to say, this was some shit a ghetto nigga like me didn't see often. He plopped down behind his desk like the boss he was, and I couldn't help but admire him. He moved like an Italian mobster from the movies, just add some dreads and change the hue. "How's Zamad doing?" he asked.

"He's good," I said while trying to parse out whether or not it was genuine.

"Okay, then what brings you my way?" he said while rubbing his goatee as his diamond-encrusted Rolex shimmered.

As I cleared my throat, a sudden moment of regret crept across me. I sat here with no money, just a handout in my father's name. I swallowed it and said, "I need your help."

He shifted in his chair immediately. "What's on your mind, fam? You like my nephew. Me and your father go way back. You don't gotta be ashamed about nothin'. This is what I'm here for."

I told him, "I'm trying to make my way, and I'm gonna have 200 grand in a few days. I only need you for a connect 'cause I'll be in need of a steady plug."

Kamar gave me a stern look, then leaned forward. "You serious, huh?"

"As a heart attack," I replied.

"What's your pops think of all this? You could have come to him, and he would have set it in order for you. I don't know, fam . . . I've been out the loop for a while now."

I studied his face as he replied, and I could sense his poker face slip for a split second, but I played along anyway.

"I know you can point me in the right direction. I'm not asking you to jump straight in headfirst. I'm not a cop or no shit like that. I'm just a hungry nigga from the hood." He laughed as I said that, so I asked him, "What's so funny?"

"You're just like your ole man. Come on, take a ride with me."

Chapter 3

(COWBOY)

Friday nights were always live in the city. I couldn't take much more of this sitting around,

"Ain't nobody heard from Zaro?" I asked while looking from Telay to Bang. As they both shook their heads I said, "Fuck this I'm 'bout to ask sis if I can use the whip. Yawl trying to slide tonight?"

"I ain't got no bread," Telay complained.

"So what? We don't need none, and we just 'bout to ride around anyway," I said while making my way to Savon's room. I pushed the door ajar and whispered, "Sis!" Her room was completely dark and I figured she was resting up for her morning shift at the hospital.

"What you want, bro, the car or some money?" she replied from the darkness.

I smiled, as she seemed to be in a good mood, so I had to try my luck with getting her car for the night. "We trying to hit up a few spots," I told Savon. We had a great relationship, and she rarely told me no for anything, especially after our mother died. She took care of me after I was released from St. Charles, IL Juvenile Department of Corrections.

"Hit the light," she said while grabbing her Birkin bag. She handed me 100 dollars and the car keys.

"Thanks, sis, I'll be back around three a.m.," I assured her.

"Just make sure I make it to work in the morning," she told me.

She worked as a CNA at St. Anthony's Medical Center. The streets wasn't her thing, and dating dope dealers was off-topic for her. Everybody in the projects was trying to get at Savon, but she didn't let that stop her from taking their money. She vowed that being a dope man's wife would not be her future; she figured it being more of a liability or a hazardous job not knowing when you'd be robbed or killed.

I pushed her Buick truck down Estate Street while we all bobbed our heads to Lil' Durk's "No Auto".

"Ride through the stage," Telay said.

I looked back at Bang in the back seat. "Tha shit rolled up yet?" I was ready to smoke some of the kush I got from Pretty Tony. The Stage was a liquor store owned by the Arabs. They sold bootlegged clothing and fake designer purses, which brought the ghetto thots out. The store was also right around the corner from Black Hawk Projects, which was ran by a vicious female named Vetta. All the ballers were cool with Sal, who was rumored to sell that Afghan heroin. The parking lot was a showcase for all the heavyweights, mostly driving exotic foreigns.

"Look at these niggas," I said, eyeing Flex in an Audi A8. I knew Mick wasn't far behind, and sure enough, they rolled up in Flex's Range Rover.

"You know you got them sticks in that muthafucka," Telay said. Whenever you see Waaco out, you could count on someone getting shot up. I went under my seat and clutched my .25 while Telay busted into laughter.

"Fuck is so funny?" I asked.

"You and that piece o' shit .25. Them niggas got switched and Dracs in the Range; what you 'gon do with tha slingshot?" Telay answered.

"Whatever, nigga," I said as I shifted my attention to a Maybach in the cut. I squinted to see if I was seeing clearly, but Zaro was definitely seated in its cabin.

"Is that Zaro?" I asked while hopping out, not waiting for a response.

I bopped over to the passenger side of the Maybach while all the bitches were jocking the car. I didn't give a fuck how it looked 'cause I was tryin' to holler at my nigga. "What's good, bro?" I said, slapping his hand.

"Shit, we chillin'. What y'all up to?" he replied nonchalantly, with a sly grin.

I nodded my head at the driver while a white Audi pulled up in sync, window to window with the drivers. Lil' Mick Nemm was behind the Audi in the Range Rover with a grimy gaze. Something didn't seem right. I touched the .25 in my pocket; I was ready. I turned to Zaro, "So what's the deal with you and those IRA muthafuckas?"

"Business as usual," he replied with an eye telling me to keep the situation on the down-low, as he obviously didn't want his boy to know what he was working on. I didn't know Kamar personally either, which made me out of pocket for divulging personal information in front of him. I cut the topic off short and switched subjects. Flex and Kamar talked for a moment, and I didn't want to be too far out the mix, so Zaro and I small-talked about nothing in particular for a bit. I did overhear Flex say they had something important to talk about later, though, whatever that meant. Flex drove away with Mick in tow.

"Unc, this is Cowboy," Zaro gave the formal introduction.

"I remember you. You're Sharon's son . . . you murked that no-good ass nigga Rodney a while back, right?" he said as I nodded my head low. I hated when people brought that up 'cause my mom has passed away now, and it brings up bad memories of what he did to her.

"Yeah, that's me," I answered shamefully.

"I was at Sharon's funeral. I'm sorry for your loss," Kamar replied while catching my facial change; you could tell he wanted to clean it up and console me, but it was too late.

"It's all good, thanks big dawg. Zaro, I'll get you later, a'ight?" I said, and he slapped hands.

I walked back to the truck, and as soon as I slid in the seat, I heard the air quake. *Blaka, laka, laka, laaaaaow blaaaaawow!* . . . everyone knew that sound; it was a switch going off. I slid the truck into gear and hauled ass out of the lot, tires screeching all around me.

"What the fuck is going on?" Telay asked, frantic.

"Shit, I don't know. I was talking to Zaro, and when I walked away niggas got to clapping," I replied, looking around as I fled the scene. I scanned for the Maybach and came up short, praying Zaro wasn't caught up in this shit.

We all spent the night at my house with Telay sprawled across the floor and Bang in his favorite spot—the bean bag chair. I stretched, then went to the living room; we had the house to ourselves, as Savon had already left for work. I looked at my phone, Instagram goin' crazy, and found out some lil' nigga named Lotto had gotten killed at the *Stage* last night. I was relieved it wasn't Zaro. I scrolled further down to a post made by Zaro, *'Had to body a nigga, what is this world coming to? smh.'*

"Damn!" I muttered, looking at the words. I scrolled down more to see if I could get more info when it hit me— Zaro posted from the hospital.

(ZARO)

I laid on the gurney looking out the window. It was taking the nurse forever to give me my discharge paperwork. The wound wasn't too bad, but I couldn't speak for the one that got killed. I'd heard he died on the operating table last night.

The events played on me heavy; last I knew, the cops had him down in homicide for the murder of the guy last night. It seemed like my plan was about to crumble before it even got the opportunity to start. I sat on the bed in deep thought, with the nurse shaking me back to reality. She walked in, looking like April from the show *Chicago Med.*

"How's that arm feeling?" she asked cheerfully, her attitude as bright as sunshine.

"It's okay, itchy a bit, but not bad," I replied.

"That's normal, I got your papers here for you to sign," she said, shuffling them to me. I needed to get out of here as quick as possible; Savon would be in any moment, and I wasn't trying to hear her out right now.

"Do you have a ride home?" she asked.

Before I could give an answer, my aunt was standing in the doorway, shaking her head.

"Please don't start, aunty," I said.

The nurse looked to Savon, "Are you going to take him home?"

"Unfortunately for him, yes," Savon replied, giving me a stare full of daggers.

We rode home in silence, and while I was happy not to hear her mouth, I had a lot more to worry about. The police had Kamar for the body, and even though he hadn't shot him, the gun was registered to him. He didn't give me a chance to say a word. I replayed the scene in my head, and all I can remember was seeing a dark figure creeping backwards, letting off wild rounds from the switch. Kamar snatched the gun from me, then put two in his chest as he lay on the ground, clinging to life.

Aunt Sheila led the way inside, and I tailed quietly, fully knowing that the moment was coming where I'd have to answer for last night. It never came. She just walked back to the kitchen and called, "You want some lunch?"

"Yes, please," I answered, hearing pots clink from the kitchen.

Vrm, vrm, vrm. My phone buzzed; it was Kamar.

"Hello?" I answered.

"What up, my G? Come by my shop tomorrow," was all he'd said.

23

I agreed, and the call ended abruptly. That was odd. I didn't know what was on his mind, but at least he wasn't in the county. I went to bathe and change clothes when my phone rang again, and it was Cowboy this time.

"Where you at?" he asked.

"At home," I replied.

"A'ight, stay there, we on our way. Aunty leave for work yet?"

"She leaving now," I said, then ended the call.

When Cowboy, Bang, and Telay got to the house, I filled them in on the IRA.

"Them niggas better be glad I couldn't get a shot off," Cowboy said, as Bang and Telay both laughed.

"What you niggas laughing at?"

"You and that dumb-ass slingshot. Which reminds me, what's the deal on the pipes? We hitting that lick or what?" Telay asked.

"Fa sho dat! I'm glad you're eager to get shit poppin', I'm waiting on the IRA. O'Riley never gave me a definite answer, but if push comes to shove, we'll use that .25 Cowboy got," I joshed. "We got to get us a striker."

I had an epiphany; I'll need to get in tune with Nylon for it to come to fruition, though. Nylon was an auto boy, and his thing was strikers and B&E. I knew we'd need him for this mission, so I said, "What y'all think about Nylon?"

"You can't be serious, that thieving-ass nigga can't help us with shit," Telay said.

"We need him to get us a striker, and I'm sure we're gonna need him to break into the house," I countered.

"If you say so, but I don't trust the dude," Telay replied. He was always the voice of reason. Bang didn't talk much; Cowboy did most of the talking for him. Cowboy himself was a radical, though; he just wanted to shine and be seen. We were all a compatible match, so I took a chance calling Nylon. He was at the house in 30 minutes. I stepped to the porch, and he was perched in the cabin of an old pickup truck with some crackhead-looking guy. Nylon hopped out the front seat and bopped to the porch with his hands in his pockets. His dreads hung shoulder-length, protecting him from the cold air, and he was slightly scrawny-looking. The kid met me on the porch, and I said, "Tell unc he can pull away, we got you."

"I told him I'd be giving him something, and when you mentioned money involved, I figured..." he said.

"Aight, I got you," I said as I pulled out a small stone from my pocket. "Give him this."

Nylon hustled over to the truck, and the man pulled away from the curb. I took him into the house, and by the time I told him the plan, he was all the way in; it didn't take much convincing at all.

Now I just hoped the IRA would have them guns in place for me...

Days later, I sat browsing Instagram on my phone. Kamar had postponed the meet, saying he had to go out of town on business. I felt like he was dodging me on the basis that I'd grabbed his gun. I don't know why I'd done it, I just reacted on impulse. I started to think this whole thing was a mistake—the IRA, Kamar, Nylon, everything. I figured I really didn't need the guns for the robbery; it was solely for once we set up shop. Even though we joked about Cowboy's .25, the fact still remained that it was all we had. As I browsed, I saw Kamar posting pics from Iran. I scoffed and knew it was a lie. This nigga out having fun. He traveled over there often, so this could be construed as business if I didn't know any better. I just shook my head.

Ding Dong!

The doorbell rang and I got up to see who it was. My aunt was at work, and I wasn't expecting anyone either. I pushed the curtains back, saw a black van out front, and through the curtains it looked like cops. I tip-toed to get a look through the peephole, and saw a nerdy, skinny white guy standing there. He almost looked like an insurance salesman, but still,

I didn't want to open the door. I just stood there, hoping he'd leave. The man wasn't budging, though, so I took a deep breath and braced myself before opening the door.

"You Zaro, mate?" he spoke with a rough Irish accent.

"Yeah, that's me," I answered. The guy looked over his shoulder at the van, and both doors slid open to reveal two biker-looking men. I stepped back right after I noticed a bulge under his shirt too.

Chapter 4

(ZARO)

I eyed the men suspiciously; the tension I had was winding down. I realized killers don't come knockin' at your door, so I eased up a bit and let my guard down. The guy broke the eerie silence.

"A friend sent us by," he said as he looked over his shoulder and signaled for the men to come over.

"A friend named who?" I questioned.

"Look, kid, I don't have time for this. He sent it, it's yours, now take it," he said sharply.

The men worked in succession to unload the tote bags from the van. All three guys lugged a tote bag each toward my porch. They pushed past me and laid the bags in the middle of my living room floor.

I was left looking down at them, unaware of what was inside. My phone buzzed... vrm, vrm, vrm. It was O'Riley.

I answered it, "Hello?"

"You got what you need?" O'Riley asked.

I cradled the phone to my ear as I opened the bags to confirm the package; I grinned at the arsenal of weapons. A sudden surge of power ran through my body—it was almost euphoric.

I smiled, "Yeah, I got 'em. Thanks. I won't let you down," I said while trying to calm my excitement.

"Don't thank me, pay me. You're 20 grand in. Call me when you take care of your business," he replied sharply and ended the call.

I scoffed, then looked down at the guns in a daze; my plan was slowly starting to formulate. I couldn't help but think about the 20 grand, though. It was a lot of money to pay. I examined one of the AR-15s.

"It's on now," I muttered with a devilish grin...

Next day . . .

I trailed behind the BMW at a slow, inconspicuous pace. Telay was busy typing on his phone, while Nylon sat in the backseat looking around at all the houses like he was in a zoo, spectating the animals in amazement. I followed the BMW into a gated community in a place called Machesney Park outside of Chicago. The car pulled into a nice two-story home.

"Damn! That mu'fuka nice!" Nylon gawked.

"Do you think it'll be a problem gettin' inside?" I inquired to Nylon.

"I don't think so. It looks pretty easy. Most of the time the doors are left open."

"What about an alarm or some shit?"

"Uhm . . . I don't know. It's hard to tell. I doubt it, though."

Telay was too focused on his phone to hear what we were plotting.

"What you think, lay?" I asked, just to see if he was paying attention.

"It's whatever with me," he said.

I chuckled, knowing he hadn't heard anything that was said.

. . . *vrm, vrm, vrm* . . . My phone buzzed again. I read the tag—Kamar. I was shocked to get a call from him at this point in my plan because I thought he was out of town.

I answered while keeping a close eye on the manager's home, "Hello?"

"I'm still out of town right now, but I'll be back next week, so stop by," he replied.

"I'm sorry about what happened. I hope that didn't cause you any hardship."

"Don't worry about that. I got that situation together, just come holla next week," he calmly replied.

"That's a bet," I said before I ended the call.

Telay rolled his head over to face me, "What we still doing sitting here?"

"I want to see who else lives here, and I'm not 'bout to go in this bitch blind. This'll only work if he has a wife or someone he cares about that we can hold hostage," I told him.

"You mean to tell me you don't know if this guy has a wife or not?"

"I do, I just want to be sure," I answered, frustrated that he was questioning me, especially after waking up out of a Telay fantasy-land trip.

"Aight, nigga, that's on you. Just don't put us in no bind," Telay replied.

The car was quiet for a moment, then a Toyota pulled into the manager's garage.

I got a good look at the woman and two kids. I'd seen what I needed to see. It was a perfect play; I pulled away.

"We can go in through that side entrance," said Nylon, pointing over my shoulder as I drove past the house slowly.

"What we doing?" Telay slurred tiredly.

I was about tired of him asking all the dumb questions . . .

"Ima let everybody know at my crib," I proclaimed before calling Cowboy.

I knew he would be happy to know the plan was unfolding, as he was a real-life action junkie. I informed him to meet me at my house, seeing as Aunt Sheila was working a double shift today, and I had the house to myself. I parked on the street. Cowboy met me in the driveway, and we all popped out in unison. After slapping hands, I led the way inside, down the basement steps, and into the lower level that was fixed up like an apartment.

"So what you want to holler about?" Cowboy asked anxiously as we descended the steps.

"I told you this nigga geeking to do some dumb shit," Telay interjected.

"Kill that shit, nigga, I ain't talkin' to you," he replied.

"Both of y'all chill out," I told them as I snaked further into the basement.

Father had it remodeled before he went to prison, but now I am the actual owner. My aunt had moved from California to watch over me during my dad's trial. My mother had been killed shortly after his trial had begun. Sheila was my legal guardian until I turned 18; I just turned 19, which meant I was on my own. I was fit for the streets, fit for whatever they came with. I keyed my way into a secret room that was camouflaged by the wood paneling of the wall. Aunt Sheila hadn't even known it was there.

As we stepped inside, everybody looked around in amazement.

"Goddamn, fam! Where did you get all this?" inquired Cowboy.

"The Irish came through for us. This shit wasn't free, so if anybody wants to back out, now's the time to do it, 'cause I'm ready to rob this bank tomorrow," I told them, then scanned everyone's faces.

I could tell Cowboy was all the way in—he already cradled one of the AR-15s. I got no rebuttal. The room was silent.

"A'ight then, I take that as we all in," I announced.

"O'Riley gave you all this?" Telay exclaimed, astonished at what he was looking at.

O'Riley had passed me an arsenal: Gen 5s, Kel-Tecs, FNs, Dracos, AR-15s (all with switches). The clips were drums, cable boxes, and a few 30s. O'Riley even threw in 10 bulletproof vests. Bang had already started fitting himself for one of the vests, and Nylon snatched up a Gen.

"We owe 20 bands for all this, so tomorrow, Telay, you and I will rob the bank; Bang, you drive; Nylon, you and Cowboy will hold the bitch hostage while we handle our thing."

"Wait a minute. I'm not babysitting shit. I want to go in the bank with y'all," Cowboy shot back.

I could tell he thought he was gonna get shorted on his cut . . .

"If it's the cut you're worried about, we all getting the same," I told him.

"I want to be in the action, don't leave me on the sideline," he complained.

"This nigga's gonna kill somebody if you put him in that bank," Telay said.

I knew he was speaking from a logical perspective, and in my view, Telay was right. Cowboy was trigger-happy, and I couldn't afford for him to send us to jail before I could get my mission off the ground. The best thing for him was to stay on the sideline—for now, that is.

"Fam, look, just do that for us. This is how it has to be for now," I replied. My tone of speech was serious so he'd get the gist of what I was saying.

He huffed, frustrated, but he was about to submit. I looked at Cowboy with pleading eyes; I didn't want to continue to argue with him.

"Ok, just know I could be valued in tight situations, my G," he replied.

We slapped hands, and the plan was in motion...

"Now all we got to do is hope the puppet don't bitch," Telay said, jokingly looking at Bang.

"Who you talking to, boy? I speak for myself," Bang shot back.

I was waiting on Cowboy to react and was shocked when he stood down; Cowboy was known for jumping in Bang's battles, as they were best friends since their time in juvie. When they met, Bang was getting pressured by some Latin Kings, and Cowboy jumped in because he despised them.

"Pull your skirt down, fam, I'm just fucking with you," Telay replied.

(ZAMAD)

Days earlier...
U.S.P BLOODY BEAUMONT
I stood in the doorway of my cell, peeping out the window.

"Chow time!" the C/O yelled.

On cue, everyone exited the unit like a hungry group of bulls—that was my signal to handle my business. I unscrewed my top light, retrieved my iPhone 13, and dialed Kamar's number.

"Yooo!" he answered.

"Was good, big dawg? I got some good news," I said.

"Let me hear it," Kamar was excited.

"I'm workin' on something that'll get me outta here real soon. I'm gonna need your help with it though."

"Okay, so what is it? You know I got you on whatever you need, dawg."

"Can you make it down here to see me this weekend?" I asked.

"I'm already there, my G. Shit, before I go, your son came by to holla at me, and we got into a little situation..."

My heart began to thud in my chest. Zaro was my only son; I couldn't allow anything to happen to him.

"What happened? Please don't tell me shit that's 'bout to ruin my day."

"Chill out, dawg, he good. He came by my office, and I think he wants me to put him on. I'm not sure exactly how,

32

but I told him I would get with him... and he did body a nigga for me," he added.

"Aw shit, how did that happen?" I asked, concerned.

"It's a long story, but the short version is some lil' punk tried to creep up, and now he's dead," he replied sharply.

I picked up what he put down, so I left the whole thing alone. It was obvious there was a lot more to the situation than what he was putting on.

"A"ight, big dawg, let me know on the visit next week." I ended the call and tucked it back into its hiding spot. The noise level inside began to rise as everyone was returning from lunch.

I stepped out of my cell onto the rail when Big Tuck came walking up.

"That Spanish nigga want you to come out to rec on the next move," he told me, almost out of breath from the walk up the steps. Tuck had weight complications; he loved to eat and couldn't wait on it.

I nodded.

"Oh shit! I almost forgot . . ." he cursed and spun around, holding a piece of chicken wrapped up in a tortilla bag. "You tryin' to buy this?"

He held up a large piece of chicken he'd stolen from the chow hall, the front of his shirt saturated in grease due to his smuggling technique.

"How much do you want?" I inquired.

"Give me a book . . . but what I really want is a piece of that good shit ya peoples got," Tuck had that dope-fiend eye going on.

He smiled as I let the question resonate with me.

"A'ight, give me the chicken, tell Trig I said to give you two. I want next week's also."

Tuck wobbled off hurriedly to find Trig, screaming his name as he walked the tier. I shook my head at how eager and happy he was to get his fix. Niggas in prison will do anything for a hit of paper spice behind these walls. Spice is a highly addictive and profitable synthetic narcotic, and I had the plug on it in other prisons.

Everyone wanted a piece of the action. I served 2 years in the SHU and met an Asian who flooded the system with illicit synthetic drugs. I went inside my cell to prepare for rec; Beaumont, Texas, was hot year-round, it made me think Texas never cooled down. I put on a pair of shorts as Trig stood at the door waiting on me; he was my personal security.

"What yard we goin' to today?" he asked.

"The middle, I got to holla at the Black Hand Popeye," I said.

"Some goin' down or something? Do I got to get that big-boy blick?" he asked, concerned.

Everyone knew when the heads of the Crips get summoned by a Black Hand to the yard, that usually meant someone was about to get dropped. I held a minister spot for T.H.F., which stood for Trigger Happy Family; we were Black Disciples, and I am what they refer to as a board member or BM for short. All the Midwest gangs were in a coalition together.

"Naw, my boi, this just some friendly business shit," I answered without stress in my tone.

Crowds of inmates congested the rec-gate, trying to get inside the yard, so I hung back to let everyone clear. I've seen too many people get stabbed that way. I looked around for Popeye and spotted him in his usual spot with two Sureños, Spookie and Shadow. They were notoriously deadly hitters for Popeye, well-trained, and not to be fucked with.

As Trig and I made our path over, Spookie turned quickly around, making the tattoos on his face appear sinister. The one across his forehead read "muerte," and he had a devil's mouth tattooed across his face that made him look morphed and animalistic.

"What's up, homes, you got some business over here?" he questioned.

It took everything in me not to put his ass in his place, but I knew Spookie was just the help. I gave Trig an eye to let me handle it, and he stepped back.

Popeye intervened. "That's no way to treat a guest, homes," Popeye said, making Spookie feel dumber than he looked.

"You needed to talk to me, and I need to speak with you as well."

"Take a walk with me," he requested.

Popeye was an older guy in his 60s. His face was scarred with pain from years of being in prison, making life-altering decisions, and a pair of thick black-framed glasses stood with those scars.

Popeye and I strolled the track with both of our security hanging 6 feet back. Popeye was shorter than I, and as with most Mexicans from Mexico, he had to look up at me as we spoke. Walking beside me, Popeye told me: "You have the best product on the yard as of today, so my people over at Victorville are looking to cop some weight if you can handle it."

"I'm sure I can accommodate . . . how much you looking to get your hands on?" I inquired.

"Like I said, it's for the homies at another spot," he moved his head in a blundering motion... "Oh, let's say 200 sheets."

I sucked my teeth; that was a pretty heavy order. Popeye knew that getting that much weight could pose a problem on top of being a threat to my pre-existing business with other institution gangs. Spice is a very lucrative business, but Popeye . . . well, he only wants the drugs for power; it isn't about the money with him. He has a life sentence and values being in control. Controlling the flow of drugs, and thus the people, can turn men into puppets.

I rolled the idea around in my head for a moment. He stared at me like an anxious child waiting for my response. I huffed, then eventually replied.

"I can possibly do that for you, but it will come with some stipulations. The first being you cannot mention my name or my involvement. Secondly, I want my cut. This can be paid on the outside with that shit y'all got that's knocking niggas in the dirt . . ."

He looked at me curiously.

"Fentanyl, that pure shit I been hearing about," I specified.

He smiled, "You want that carfentanil . . . it's the highest purity. You are aware that shit is very dangerous, and you'll have to be careful with whomever's hands you put it in."

"I'm fully aware of that. I have a friend that will help me, he's a veteran in the game," I explained.

"What's the price on the sheets? And don't give me that thousand dollar per clip bullshit routine," he asked.

"Well, I do have someone else that I have to answer to financially, so if your price can match for the fentanyl, I'm sure I can do 450 a sheet, especially if you're getting the whole 200 every whoop," I told him.

"That's fine by me, let's get this ball rolling."

"I'll call my people today and line it up, give me the address you're using or a phone number," I replied.

He scribbled on a piece of paper and handed it to me . . . "Call this number, tell them Popeye gave you it and they'll set you up with whatever you need."

"Okay, but what's the ticket on the fentanyl?" I asked.

"Read the paper," he muttered.

I looked at the paper, and the price he wrote, needless to say, was one that made me smile.

"One more thing, jefe," I spurted.

"Anything, what is it?" he answered.

I looked around suspiciously and made sure no one could hear what I was about to ask.

"I'll throw in an extra 200 sheets if you can drop someone for me," I secreted the words carefully.

"Who is it, migo?" he whispered.

"Red."

His eyes widened. Red was a BM for the Gangster Disciples and one of my comrades; this conversation was enough to get me and my men ex-ed out of every prison yard in America.

"I'll do that for you, migo."

Chapter 5

Days later...

Amy sat in tears beneath the blindfold. Her home had been taken over by people she didn't know, and her main concern, her children, were locked away somewhere else in their own room. I paced back and forth, anticipating the manager's return to the house. Telay and I were in the dining room with the sniffling woman while Nylon had watch on the kids. Cowboy and Bang would arrive once they got the call that we had the manager.

"What is this all about?" Amy asked, frightened.

"You'll find out soon enough once your husband gets home," I replied in an easing tone to calm her agitation.

"We don't have any money here. You got the wrong house," she pleaded.

I had to chuckle; if only she knew... "What time does he normally get home?" I asked.

"Soon," she said sharply.

Suddenly, the garage door activated. Telay jumped to attention, and both our movements synced as we moved to the door to catch him off guard on his way in. The move was calculated and precise. As the door opened, I gripped my G19. He entered slowly.

"Girls, where are you?" he called out, carrying two teddy bears; he hadn't a clue of what was to come.

I crept behind him slowly, then put the 19 to his head. "Don't move or you and your entire family will die here today," I hissed, every word slow to make my point.

The man raised his hand in defeat. Telay popped out from his perch slowly, with his weapon drawn. Telay had him from the front, so together we had him boxed in. We had on our Pooh Shiesty masks, so it made us look like venomous snakes. The man was completely shaken up by our presence.

"What is it that you want? We don't have any money here," he spoke.

"I've heard that one before, but fortunate for you, your job does," I assured him.

I walked him further inside so he could see his wife was bound to a chair in the dining room. Instantly, the wind was knocked out of him, and he took a deep sigh. "Please don't do this to us," he begged.

"It's already done, so take a seat next to your wife," I commanded.

Telay tied him to the chair using zip ties, then blindfolded him so we didn't have to keep our masks on. I called Cowboy and Bang to give them our location.

"I got a proposition for you, Mr. Bank Guy. What's your name?"

"Roger Martin," he wavered.

"Okay, Roger, I want your help robbing that bank tomorrow. I'm gonna hold your wife and kids while we get it done safely. You think you can help me with that?" I propositioned.

"I don't know; they have all sorts of hidden security measures that I have no control of."

"Just do as he says so we can get through this," Amy interjected.

"Listen to your wife, Roger. We will kill you if this plan is not taken seriously . . ."

Right after I spit out the word, Telay led Bang and Cowboy in, escalating the threat of violence further.

"Somebody call the cavalry?" Cowboy said.

Upon hearing other voices in the room, Roger knew he was trapped. As I went over my plan with him, Amy whimpered softly.

Later that night...

I was parked in darkness, a quarter block up from Fast Cars, a car lot that sold high-end, fast vehicles. I watched as Nylon hopped the fence and snaked his way through the cars before I lost sight of him . . .

5 minutes later . . . screeches, an all-black Trackhawk careened out the parking lot. It sounded like a lion roared as it sped past me; Nylon rode that lion as if it was in the Kentucky Derby. I bolted up in my seat, mashed the gas pedal, and pushed Amy's Nissan truck to its max in order to catch up with the Striker. We made it to Roger's home, with plans to rob the bank in the morning at 10:30 a.m., after they received the first drop. Roger had given some good intel on the bank, but my plans weren't to be a perfect banker robber; I wanted power in the streets . . .

(COWBOY)

11:00 A.M. Friday morning...

I paced aimlessly back and forth; if Amy could feel my stare, I'd have burned a hole in her. I was trying to figure out exactly what needed to be done, especially as Amy's life was hanging in the balance. Zaro had said they would be in the bank for only 2 minutes, but it's going on thirty now, and I'm wrestling with thoughts of killing her and getting the hell out of dodge. I didn't even know if the cops were on their way, but nonetheless, Zaro should have called by now to let me know they were safe. My thoughts ran rampant, and Nylon popped into the room.

"You a'ight, fam?"

"Hell naw," I said, nodding towards the kitchen, subtly hinting we were within Amy's earshot.

"What's up, my nigga?" he said in a hushed tone.

"Man, I'm 'bout to kill this bitch. Zaro should have called by now."

"Damn, you right. I hadn't paid much attention to the time . . . you think they got caught or something?"

"Nigga, I don't know, but I don't wanna be a sitting duck for the twelve . . . you feel me?!"

"Then what do we do?"

I shook my head. Nylon looked to me for answers, but I was at a loss.

I huffed. "Let's give them 10 more minutes. Search the house for anything we can take so it won't be a blank mission, and if he doesn't call by then, I'll kill the bitch myself."

Those were the magic words for his inner thief, and as he went on the hunt, I followed suit. When I stepped back into the dining room, Amy must've felt my presence.

"You guys should've been out my house by now, what's the hold-up?" she asked.

"How do you figure that? We're right on schedule," I lied to keep her from doing something out of panic or fear of dying.

"I can feel something amiss. My husband will do his part. Don't kill us. Your friend's plan may have gone to shit for reasons that have nothing to do with any of us," she replied.

"We'll be on our way soon. Have no worry."

10 minutes had passed, still no call. Nylon and I met back up in the kitchen; he had all types of shit in his hands . . .

"Did they make the call yet?" he asked.

I shook my head. "No. Start putting that shit in ol' girl's car. We got to get rid of her," I said somberly.

"What about the kids? You gone murk them too?"

"Hell naw, I'm not that cold."

"Why would you do her, if she hadn't seen our faces?" Nylon said.

His statement did make sense. However, she heard our voices, and who's to say she didn't get a peek under the blindfold? I was wrestling with these thoughts in my brain, and after moments of going back and forth with my conscience, I realized this bitch had to go; the jury rendered its verdict. I looked at the time—Zaro was 45 minutes late on the call.

I eased into the dining room where Amy sat, bound to the chair. I wanted to take her by surprise, as I was about to kill her in cold blood. I gripped the G19, then pointed it to her head. I honestly didn't want her to talk me out of it; the real reason for my surprise attack. I bit my bottom lip, my finger rested on the hair trigger—5 pounds of pressure and we would be on our way . . . my mind was racing.

"Who's there?" she said, moving her head from side to side.

The grim reaper hovered over her with his scythe drawn, ready to capture her soul. My finger eased harder on the trigger. *BOOM!* A single shot echoed throughout the house. I bolted for the door, and Nylon and I made a speedy getaway.

(ZARO)

10:45 A.M. Lawndale Bank...

I slung the book bag of money over my shoulder. Telay covered the people on the floor with his Draco, sweeping the room as we eased toward the exit of the bank. We were almost free and clear. So much had happened before we robbed the bank, with the truck arriving late, pushing the time we went in later, but now it was almost over. The manager was fully cooperative; he'd helped us hit the piggy safe hard. We were 6 feet from the door as the sun beamed upon our exit, like the lights of heaven shining upon us . . .

"Drop the weapon," an armed man said, wielding his gun at me.

I looked at him in total shock. Where had he come from? What outfit was he? As I stared at him, though, it became apparent that he was an off-duty cop when I glimpsed his gun holster.

"Put the gun down, kid. I'm an off-duty gang officer," he said.

Telay and I both were frozen with fear; there was no way out. I thought about having a shoot-out, but that would only add to the damage. As I slowly started to lower my gun . . . *TISH!*

The lobby's front window's glass crashed in. Bang crashed the Striker through the lobby as the cop ducked for cover; it gave Telay and me a chance to run to the jeep.

SKERRRRRRK! The tires screeched as they spent their tread getting us out of the parking lot. Bang weaved the truck. *BLOCKA! BLOCKA! TISH!* Shots were fired, shattering the back window . . .

"AH, fuck!" I yelped. I felt something punch me in my back.

"What happened?" Bang asked, looking over at me.

"I've been shot. I felt around to see if it went through my vest... I'm good," I replied, looking over my shoulder.

The dashboard read 90 mph as we fled the scene. Suddenly, I heard sirens in the distance.

"They on us, try to get to the highway. We can lose them faster," I said.

Bang merged on I-90 so they wouldn't be able to tell if we'd lost them on the way to Chicago or if we were still in town. The Striker moved like a bolt of lightning down the highway; it felt like I was in a rocket. The sirens had gotten fainter as time went by. Bang loved to play GTA on his PS, and when I looked at him, he had the same look he gets when playing. This was the reason I wanted him to drive; I felt if the situation presented itself as it did, we would get away better.

"Exit on Harrison, then hit the West End. We can hide out at the motel," I said.

It looked like we had gotten away; I pulled my phone out to call Cowboy and let him know they could leave the house. My phone was trashed—the screen was smashed from being hit with a bullet. I looked back at Telay as he was unzipping the backpack of money.

"My phone is cracked, we gotta call Cowboy and let him know they can leave the house."

Telay chuckled, "If you know ya boi like I know him, baby dead by now," Telay remarked.

"Let's hope not . . ."

Moments later, Bang was at the door, so I picked up the room phone to call Cowboy. We talked briefly, and I let him know our location. "Cowboy and Nylon on their way here now," I said after ending the call.

We all sat in silence on the bed and waited on the rest of the team to arrive to count the money. 20 minutes later, a car pulled up in front of the room. Then the car door slammed, and I jumped to see who it was.

"Cowboy and Nylon," I said, then opened the room door.

Cowboy walked in animated, shaking his head... "Why the fuck you ain't call, fam? I thought y'all got caught up or something."

"We almost did, ya boi Bang put them on a high-speed and I got shot," I said.

"Dam, for real. Where 'bout?" Cowboy inquired.

"In the back, but the vest got it. Good thing O'Riley gave up them vests."

"The million-dollar question is, what you do 'bout the broad?" Telay asked.

We all looked at him for his response . . . "What does it matter?" he replied.

(ROGER)

1 hour later at Lawndale Bank...
I sat in my office with my head down, I'd been trying to call Amy since the robbery was over. I hoped my love was still alive, but the odds weren't in my favor. *Knock! Knock!* Someone tapped on my door. I looked up to see two detectives. I signaled for them to come in and waited for the questioning to start.

"Mr. Procter, I'm Robbery and Homicide Detective Abotts, and this is my partner Coats. We need you to answer a few questions if you would. We know this is a rough time, but we need to get some things clear," he said, then pulled out a note pad.

"What can I do for you, fellas," I replied, my eyes still puffy and red.

"The robbers came straight for you. Some of your co-workers says it almost look like you helped them rob the vault," Abotts accused.

"That's preposterous. There's no truth in that. What would give someone that idea?" I said, slightly embarrassed.

"None of the dye packs were taken, and the sterilized bills hadn't been touched. It was almost as if you told them what to take or possibly even gave it to them. The really odd thing is, how did they know you were the manager?" Abotts inquired further.

I felt stupid. The cop was making some valid points, and I had no rebuttal. All I wanted to do was make sure my family was okay, and I couldn't let these cops know anything if they were still at my home.

"Look, detective, I can assure you I had nothing to do with this robbery. I've been working at this branch for ten years, and I would never jeopardize my livelihood."

"Uhm!" Abotts remarked then looked around . . . "Maybe you got yourself in a bind with gambling . . . or maybe some drugs? It looks like you were crying."

"I just had a gun put in my face," I replied.

"Roger, we can help you if you allow us to," detective Abotts said.

He was really pressing hard, and I was running out of things to say. His partner—Coats—just kept staring in my direction, giving me an eerie feeling, as if he wanted my soul for harvesting. Abotts was a fat, overweight slob, while Coats was the total opposite—military straight-up jarhead-type. He made me feel like I failed my bank, and I couldn't wait for it all to be over so I can go home to my wife and kids. After a long while of back-and- forth, it was finally over. Abotts handed me his card and exited my office.

I drove home like a bat out of hell, praying my family was okay. I whipped into the driveway, the car still rolling as I hopped out. Amy's car was gone. I ran to the door, my heart thudding in my chest, beads of sweat covering my face. As I reached the door, I noticed it wasn't locked . . .

"Amy!" I yelled out as I ran through the house . . .

I noticed the house was in total disarray, and I could smell gun powder in the air. I feared the worst, but standing the living room, I was completely confused.

"Roger, is that you?" she yelled back at me from upstairs.

I hurriedly ran up and found my family huddled up in the corner of my attic. I ran and gave them a tight hug.

"Daddy, daddy we're scared," my beautiful little girls said in unison.

"Roger, what happened at the bank? I watched the news. They said it was an awful situation."

"It was. The cops think I had something to do with it so we have to get out of here," I gasped, out of breath from adrenaline.

I gathered my family up. We ransacked the house for clothes and whatever else we needed, and left to take a trip for a while. I fumbled through the cabinets looking for my stash of Percocet . . .

"Fuck!" I muttered; they were gone, but I did have clue of what to do now.

No one knew of my drug habit or the fact I was a gambler. I stood in the kitchen to get my bearings together, then met Amy and the kids at the front door with all our travel belongings. The kids were all packed and ready, and Amy looked up to me and asked:

"Where are we going?"

That was a very good question because I had no clue either. It finally hit me: the Goldstar Motel on the west end of town. I hadn't been there in some time, but it was the perfect place to hide and was far enough from the city. That's where I could get my bearings straight; there was still the situation of needing some money to buy more drugs, but I knew just where to get it...

"Everybody head to the car, I know of a nice motel on the west side of town. I just gotta make one quick stop," I said, as if I had the situation under control. Truth was, I didn't even remotely, but I couldn't let that fear show towards my family.

As I pulled into the *Lucky 7* pub, the thought of playing a little cards for money came to mind. I had to look at my family to stay focused. My kids needed me, and I was in no place to do anything stupid. I looked at Amy and kissed her. "Wait here, I'll be right back," I said while staring into those beautiful eyes.

"I hope you're not going in there to do anything stupid, Roger," she remarked.

I chuckled. "No, I gotta get us some money. O'Riley will front it to me."

"Roger, those guys in there are trouble. If you step into that bar, that's what you're gonna get," she said.

She was right; nonetheless, I defied her request and stepped out the car . . .

***

47

(ZARO)

Later the same night WAACO...

We split the money up in Cowboy's bedroom while Savon and Tiffany were watching TV in the other room. This was the perfect time to go over my plan; everybody was laid back and in the zone— except for Cowboy, as usual.

"Man, I'm 'bout to go buy me a Hellcat tomorrow!" he said, full of excitement.

"Fam, dub that shit down, my nigga, we got to stick to the script," I said.

"Nigga, all this bread we got right now, that shit was too easy! We can hit another bank," he replied.

I couldn't believe how stupid this nigga was; everything we talked about went in one ear and out the other.

"Told you this nigga is an action junky. I'm not robbing banks for the rest of my life, that ain't me, my boi," Telay interjected.

"Me neither. We got 30 thousand a piece after I pay the IRA. Kamar gone get at me this week, and we can piece this shit together. I'm sure he'll give us a plug, but if not, I'm gonna talk to my dad," I said.

"Psst, nigga, yo da got L in da feds, fuck is he gone do for us? Not to mention Kamar is out of town," Cowboy replied arrogantly.

"Don't be stupid," I said, then stared at him like he was crazy.

Bang and Nylon just sat and listened. I could tell they were up for it all, though Nylon didn't know the full extent of what I had planned.

"Y'all got me confused, put me up on game," Nylon asked.

I shifted my gaze toward him... "We about to take the city over, beginning with these Waaco niggas," I said, then looked him in the eye to get a read on him.

"I'm down for whatever . . . I got these out of Roger's house," Nylon said, then held up a Ziplock bag full of pills. I grabbed the pills from him and gave them a thorough examination. It had to contain at least 300 OC 80mg's. Cowboy looked at him menacingly . . . "You said you ain't find shit in the house, why you lie?" he asked, upset.

"I forgot I had them, for real. The rush of all this money took over my thoughts. Not to mention I don't even know what that shit is," he replied.

"Dope, nigga, and a lot of it."

"We can prolly get another 20 grand for the pills or sell them ourselves," I reasoned.

It was obvious Cowboy's blood was boiling, and I could see the steam emanating from his skull.

"Whatever I got to do, I'm all the way in. I wouldn't have shit right now if it wasn't for you niggas," Nylon said.

"Start by putting your 30 bandz in my hands; let me help make you it grow. Or you stay in one spot looking dumb," I said, then shifted my stare at Cowboy . . .

He knew I was on his top about the situation...

He huffed as he paced the floor, shaking his head like a baby.

"What we doing?" he asked, frustrated.

"My nigga, first thing I want to do is blow that nigga Mick down. Without him and their nigga Calico, Waaco ain't shit," I said.

"Facts," Telay replied.

"Tomorrow, I'm gonna get with the IRA and see if they got some product we can move until I meet up with Kamar."

"And what if that don't happen?" Cowboy asked.

"I'm not worried about that, my boi, I put a nigga down for him. Real recognize real, fam."

I stepped out the room to take a quick piss and ran into Tiffany coming out the bathroom... "What's up, Tif?" I said. She looked me up and down, then walked off.

"What was that all about?" I thought to myself, then stepped in the bathroom.

***

Next day—LUCKY 7 PUB...
"Zaro, it's good to see you," O'Riley greeted me and shook my hand.

I took a seat next to him and laid a big envelope full of money on the table. O'Riley eyed the package suspiciously . . .

"Is that for me?" he asked with a greedy grin.

"20 grand, all hundreds," I replied.

He leaned back in his seat, opened the envelope, and examined the money. His gaze suddenly changed, and he slid the money back towards me. I looked at him confused.

"I can't accept that right now," he said.

"I don't understand. This is what you told me. 20 grand. What's the problem?"

He pulled his phone out and typed in some words. Moments later, he showed me the screen playing WREX local news from yesterday, with footage of the bank robbery. He turned the phone back around and put it in his bomber jacket.

"You catch my drift? That money smells filthy," O'Riley said.

Marty sat and stared at me. He hadn't said a word since I walked in. I was speechless. I didn't know what to say until I remembered the pills we had. "Then how about 300 OC 80mg's?" I asked.

"Listen, I ain't in a rush to get the money. You got time to pay. Your deadline isn't here yet. You've only owed me for two days. I got those pills myself; in fact, they may have come from me. You should pay your dad's friend Kamar a visit."

I grabbed the money, stuffed it in my pants, and rose to leave. We shook hands, and I exited the bar, soon to return . . .

Chapter 6

(FLEX)

Shareef's Diner—same day...

I slung the Amiri backpack over my shoulder as I left the back entrance of Shareef's diner. I opened the door to my Audi, threw the bag in Remo's lap, and, as he stashed it between his legs, I pulled off. It was time to put our product in the projects.

"He say this shit laced with that carfetanil, so be careful with it," I said.

"Nigga, I'm the chemist, this what I do, fam," Remo replied arrogantly.

"I'm just saying, we don't want to kill all our customers," I said.

Remo and I were business partners; the nigga was slicker than oil, and our combination of skills made us a team. I had the plug, and he had the knowledge of the bag. Together, we had the city screaming Waaco with his perfect blend of dope. I drove to the back building in Waaco, where we shook all the dope. Remo slung the bag over his shoulder and headed inside. I hopped out the whip, then got into the Range Rover. Lil' Durk's death ain't easily forgotten. Moments after, Calico and Lil' Mick emerged. Calico slid in the front with Mick hopping in the back. We slapped hands, and I pulled out the projects.

"What's the deal, big dawg, what we doing?" Calico asked.

"I got to handle some shit with them ISG niggas," I replied, uneasy about my dealings with them.

Calico shook his head.

Calico and I moved to Rockford from Chicago a few years back. We were tighter than virgin pussy and came up robbing niggas when we caught a body together. He stuck to the code, so I had to respect his gangster, and from that point on, we were ride or die tight. To find the plug on heroin, I met Kamar and Zamad, and then through them, I met the Muslim guy, Shareef.

Calico was my right hand, and Remo was just an asset. I had to keep him at bay, thinking we were business partners though, until I'm able to get rid of him. I'll probably have Calico put a bullet in him. I hopped on the highway; Indiana was a 3-hour trip. The car was silent for a while until Calico turned the music down . . .

"What we 'bout to get into?" he asked.

"Remember a couple of nights ago Kamar murked the lil' nigga?" I asked... Lil' Mick interrupted from the back seat.

"Kamar ain't kill that nigga, Zaro did. Kamar just took the beef for it," Mick proclaimed.

"What you mean? You seen something different than what everybody sayin'?" I asked.

"Fucking right, Kamar snatched the pipe from him soon after he blew him down. Kamar just made sure he was dead in front of everyone."

I sighed . . . "It don't even matter, we got to get rid of the nigga Mikey. He put the lil' up to doin' it, and I paid for the hit," I explained.

"Fam, why you ain't come to me with that shit?" Calico asked.

"Because, if that nigga find out it was me, he'll cut my water off. You know him and Shareef is tight; he got that half-bred Afghan mufuka under his thumb."

I pulled off on the first exit to 'Gary.' As we drove through the slums of the city, I took my phone out to call Mikey, and he answered the first ring . . .

52

"You in my city, big dawg?" he asked.

"Yep, meet me at this Red Roof Inn off the highway," I said, then ended the call and looked over to Calico.

"Dumbass nigga think he 'bout to get some paper when he pull up and put his goofy ass in the ground," I said.

We sat in the parking lot waiting on Mikey to show up. He finally pulled in, driving a small Toyota with someone in the passenger seat with him. I squinted my eyes to see who it was and shook my head.

"What now?" Calico asked, seeing the same interruption I saw.

I thought for a minute while he parked. As he hopped out the car, I made out the passenger with him: some cute, light-skinned female. I dunno why she was with this bum-ass nigga, I thought to myself as I signaled for him to follow me. Before he could exit his vehicle, we both pulled out into traffic in tandem. I turned to Mick with a menacing stare and spoke, "Switch both of they asses off when we park. You got it?" He nodded.

I parked in front of a vacant, boarded-up house—a perfect place with no witnesses or nothin', as the whole block was a ghost town. As he parked the small Toyota behind me, I glued my eyes to the rearview. He leaned in, gave the female a kiss, and before he could get the door open, Mick was there. He'd tiptoed out the back seat with the Gen5 and sprayed the car with 50 rounds in a split second. *Fa! Fa! Fa! Fa! Fa! Fa! Fa!* The block sounded like a helicopter was hovering overhead. Mick slid back into the back seat, and we drove back to Rockford, listening to "Sleazy Flow" by Sleazworld Go.

(O'Riley)

Two days later...

Marty and I sat at the bar top running a game of Tuck and conversating.

"What do you think of Zamad's kid?" Marty said, then laid down a spread.

"I think he can be valued for what we're trying to do. This could be our ticket away from Curly, and he'll draw Kamar out of that rock he's been hiding under," I answered.

"Zaro will be a valued asset, especially once we get the motion going with Bruiser," Marty stated.

Bruiser was the lead biker for the Devils Angels in Chicago; they ran methamphetamine and other drugs from Mexico once a month. Bruiser had an idea to spread the meth through Rockford and Chicago at a time when meth was only prominent in select states, not Illinois. Bruiser thought it would be a goldmine for his gang, but he needed our help with distribution. The blacks were in control of the drug market, but that would put us back in power.

"We will cripple Flex on the west end. Make them two monkeys take each other out, it's clear the kid has a chip on his shoulder though. He has some sort of vendetta against Flex."

Marty nodded. *Vrm, vrm, vrm* . . . my phone buzzed.

"Speak of the Devil," I said, looking at the tag.

"Who is it?" Marty asked.

"Curly," I said, then read his message.

"What does he want?"

"To meet," I said, then rose from my seat and laid my cards on the table.

"You need me to go with you?"

Curly was the only person in this world that made me nervous due to the fact that he held power over Marty and me.

"Yeah, I need you to come with me, mate. The cocksucker creeps me out, guy gives me the chills when he's around," I said as Marty laughed. We got our coats and exited the bar to meet Curly.

Sinnissippi Park was our meeting spot; the place was beautiful in the fall, with the leaves on the trees turning all sorts of beautiful colors. Not many people would be there either, at least criminals that is, so it was a spot no one in our world frequented. As I pulled my F-150 into the parking stall, I looked around for Curly, and he was nowhere to be found.

"This guy's always late," Marty complained.

"Cocksucker thinks he runs this city," I replied, shaking my head...

Then a black Impala pulled into the park, and I leaned up in my seat... "That's him," I stated.

He parked the Impala window to window next to my truck. The window eased down slow...

"Detective Curly Abotts, how's it going?" I asked, just needed to stroke his ego a bit.

His partner, Coats, sat in the passenger seat. The two were like Miami Vice cops, only Abotts was sloppy and Coats was the square guy.

"I need a bit of information that I'm sure you're able to help me with," he said.

"Okay, shoot it at me."

"The Lawndale Bank job. You know something about those high-powered guns? Looked like they could've come from some of your IRA buddies," Abotts proclaimed.

I paused to think if I should give Zaro the strikeout now or later as planned. He was still 20 grand in with me at this time, not to mention Flex was still in the way. Abotts and Coats were aggressive, they knew that I knew some of those guns did come from me, and I was on their payroll, which meant I had to say the right thing. From this point on, he would not hear anything other than my submission or he'd haul us off to jail with all the shit they had on our heads.

"Let Marty and I put our ear to the streets. There is this kid that just showed up, it's Zamad's son. We don't have nothin' solid for you, but in time I'm sure we will," I said, hoping that would keep the sharks at bay...

Coats and Abotts both looked at each other at the mention of Zamad's name . . .

"You think his kid's trying to follow his pops' footsteps?" Coats asked.

"I don't know, let me find out for you," I replied.

"Okay, you two will report back in two weeks. And one other thing, what do you know about this guy?" Abott said, then handed me a folder containing an 8x10 still photo . . .

I looked at the photo and chuckled, then passed the photo to Marty.

"You know this prick?" he asked sarcastically.

"He's a fucking bum, name's Roger. He's 30 grand in with me right now. What's to him?" I asked curiously.

"We think he may have helped rob the bank," Coats interjected.

"If he did, he's playing the game pretty good. The guy came and got some from me 2 days ago," I answered, then handed the photo back to the detectives.

We parted ways, and Marty and I drove back to the pub in silence. Curly Abotts and Coats had sent us on our mission. Hated dealing with the two cops, but they had us on a slew of charges that could put us away for life. We'd been paid informants for a little over 20 years. It was Marty and I who put Zamad in prison; we introduced him to his wife, who helped put him inside. She was a dark-skinned half-breed, and he fell in love and had a baby with her before she was murdered. She never even got a chance to testify at the trial, as she was murdered right before. Zamad never made us for informants though; no one has since then either.

The IRA was not a war of our dealings with the cops. If they knew any of this, they'd have our heads. O'Mally was head of the council, and he could see through walls, so we had to be careful how we moved. I pulled up at the pool hall where Bruiser's gang hung out. Bruiser was a long-bearded, barely built guy with hair as long and brittle as Jesus. Bruiser was hardcore; he's killed with his bare hands, giving him his name. He looked up from the pool table as we walked in and smiled... "O'Riley, what brings you fellows down here with us trash?" he said in a raspy biker tone.

"We want you to help us open that meth line on the southside," I replied.

"I thought you boys had a bunch of monkeys jumping in your bed," he looked around the room, then laughed a fit; all his comrades joined in, of course.

"We got the answer to our problem. O'Mally wants to use the Lucky 7 as the point of distribution," I told him.

"We're good with that. My guys are headed to Mexico this week. Get your boys together and we will make sure everyone is on the same page," Bruiser replied.

I nodded, we shook hands, then Marty and I were on our way. I called O'Mally and had him set up a meeting with the IRA council.

(COWBOY)

Bloomingdale's Mall, Bloominton, IL—same day...

Bang and I skulked through the mall looking for outfits. We had a little money to blow, and Zaro said we could splurge a little bit.

"After we leave here, I wanna hit up the car lot. I seen some nice shit on our way here," I said.

"That's cool, but Zaro said no big purchases, remember," Bang replied.

"I know what he said, and a car ain't no big purchase."

As we walked through the mall, Tiffany was casually strolling with Flex; she had an arm full of bags herself, but her expression changed when she looked up and saw me. I was only fucking her ugly ass. It was Telay who liked her, so she didn't have to turn her head from me. Flex nodded at me with a smirk...

"You see that? Tiffany's black ass ain't shit now that she fucking Flex. Just like that Pac song 'I Get Around,'" Bang said, then we both busted a gut.

"I can't wait till we take Waaco over. All the hoes gone be on all of us, ya feel me?" I said.

"I know, me too, mu'fukas gone see us out here shining, my nigga," Bang said.

"Yeah, but is you gone bust that switch to get it? Because the niggas not 'bout to let us get in this game for free. We gone have to lay the murder game down; can you stomach that?"

"I'm all in, my boi. This shit ain't nuffin'," Bang said with confidence.

"We gone see, just don't bitch up when they turn up the heat."

Bang and I walked a while longer, then left the mall to find the car lot back in Rockford.

"They got some cheap cars," Bang stated as we pulled into Rice's Auto Sales. "So what you gonna cop?"

"Something simple. I'm not trying to do nothing flashy, just something low-key that we can trap around in. You feel me?" I said, then we both popped out the car.

As we walked around the lot slowly, the sales clerk eventually approached.

"Can I help you boys with anything today?" the clerk asked. We came up on a nice 20' Charger, with the tag reading only 15 thousand miles. It was out of our individual price range, but Bang and I split the check since we were together perpetually anyway.

"Y'all take cash?" I asked. The guy looked around cautiously, like he was gonna do us a favor.

"I'm sure we can make accommodations for you if you have it now."

I pulled the roll of money from my pocket, and within an hour, Bang and I were racing down the highway, switchin' lanes.

As we pulled into Waaco, all the guys standing outside gawked at us, though not admiring the car necessarily, but making sure we weren't no opps. The sun was setting, and darkness was creeping in. Bang and I hopped out our whips. Bang tailed me in my sister's Toyota. As we lugged the bags towards our building, no one was standing outside as usual, but it was almost odd until we entered and saw Mick sitting on the steps in darkness.

"Where that bitch-ass nigga Zaro?" he asked viciously.

He caught me off guard with the question, Mick never asked about Zaro. We were nobodies to Waaco goons; they looked at us as non-entities.

"Fuck if I know, he ain't in my pocket. What you need with him?" I asked curiously. He stood up from his perch and walked towards me...

"Give him this for me," he said, then pulled out a gun. *Boc! Boc! Boc!* . . . "AH shit!" I yelped while falling backwards.

Bang pulled out with lightning speed and fired back...

(BANG)

The gun jerked in my hand as I shot back. *Fa! Fa! Fa! Fa! Fa!* Cowboy stumbled backwards as Mick fired in our direction. His gun must've jammed or something, because he took off running. All I could remember was Cowboy asking me if I would bust my gun. I gave chase out the building, firing at Mick. *Fa! Fa! Fa! Fa! Fa!*

Once I lost sight of him, I began to fire blind shots. As I came up on the back parking lot though, I saw him run to the Range Rover, and it was evident that trouble was coming. Calico popped out with a Type 56. *Fi! Fi! Fi! Fi! Fi! Fi! Fi!* As sparks flew into the night air, I spun around and ran back towards the building to help Cowboy. When I reached the building, the door stood open and Cowboy was gone. I looked around the first floor, then thought maybe he'd gone home. When I walked up the stairs, I noticed him on the ground, bleeding out, and kneeled down next to him.

"Cowboy, you good, fam?" I asked, but got no response.

I pulled out my phone from my jacket and called 911, just as Savon stepped out from the apartment and screamed, seeing her brother on the ground.

"What the fuck happened? Oh my god, don't tell me he dead!" she screamed frantically.

"Tha, tha, tha lil' nigga Mick . . . he, he, he, sha, shot him," I said, stuttering. It's something I did whenever I was nervous or scared.

Cowboy lay in my arms, bleeding out.

"Did you call 911?" Savon asked.

"Yes," I answered, shaking my head, tears streaming down my face.

"Why did he do this?" Savon asked between her own sobs.

She looked down at the Gen 5 in my hand . . . "If the police are on their way, you need to go hide that."

I ducked into the apartment and put the gun away, and when I returned, I could hear the wailing of paramedics and police cars.

"Why did he do this?" Savon asked for the second time.

"I don't know. We came in and he just got to throwing at him."

The ambulance showed up quickly, but a crowd of people had already started to form. There were murmurs in the crowd inquiring if he was alive and speculating what happened. They loaded him into the ambulance while giving him chest compressions.

"Is he alive?" I asked.

"Sir, step back and let us do our job," the lady said as they loaded him in the back and closed the door. The ambulance screamed off, with Savon and the paramedics tailing it, which left me behind to answer to the police.

Chapter 7

(ZARO)

Kamar's car lot in East State that same night . . .

I gaped at all the expensive cars while Telay and I waited in the front lobby. He had all the high-end cars I dreamed to see myself in. Tonight, I was here on business though, nothing more. Kamar stepped out from the back room looking saucy; it was a different type of saucy from what I was accustomed to though. He was dressed more like Jay-Z than a model from a GQ mag.

"Zaro, I'm glad to see you made it over. Sorry to call you over so late, can't be too cautious these days. So, who is this?" he asked, diverting his attention to Telay.

"This my best friend Telay," I explained.

Kamar stuck his hand out for a shake . . .

"Let me talk to your homie in private. Chris here can show you some of the nice cars on the lot," Kamar said.

Chris walked up in sync with our conversation . . .

"You ever see what the inside of a Lambo look like?" Chris asked Telay.

Telay looked to me as if to ask if it was okay. I nodded, and Kamar and I walked off. He closed the door to his office behind him.

"A young boss in the making, I see," Kamar said, then took a seat behind his desk.

There was a brief silence before he spoke, "I want to say good lookin' out on putting that lil' nigga down for me," he said.

"That wasn't nothing," I reassured him.

"I talked to your dad, told him you came by."

"With all due respect, I'm not a kid anymore. I came to you to be treated like a man, and I got my own money. So, can you help me?" I said.

"I ain't gone beat around the bush. Imma do that for you, but I'm going out on a limb with this, and if you fuck this up, it's not gonna be your ass, it's both of ours. These are the kind of people you can't underestimate. You know what I mean by that?" he asked with narrow, piercing eyes.

I nodded my head. I didn't know exactly what he meant, but I understood his point.

"That's a question, my boi," he reiterated.

"Uhm, I don't quite understand, but I can handle anything that comes my way. I'm a street nigga, fam, we out here," I said finally.

He smiled. I knew he was about to say something tantalizing.

"These ain't them street niggas that y'all used to. These guys are on another level of violence, so tread lightly with them," he said as he scribbled something on a piece of paper... "Pull up here tomorrow and tell him you my nephew. He already expectin' you."

"Thanks, unc."

"Don't thank me, just make that shit happen. Oh, one more thing, your old man wanted me to give you something. I've been holding onto this mufuka since he went to jail," he said and rose from his seat... "Follow me."

We went to the garage to a 2006 Magnum just sitting there. I tilted my head, looking at it curiously.

"Unc, it's a nice car and all for that era, but it's 2025, gang," I explained.

He laughed lightly at my remark, then got inside and started the engine. It growled like a lion, and I twisted my face in amazement.

"It's called a Hellafant, one of the fastest engines in America right now. This a red key, lil' one," Kamar said, with an arrogant smile.

The car was almost magical. It was a fully 2025 digital touch screen all the way through, and as we walked around the back, he popped the hatch and pulled the panel from the side, revealing a screen. He put a code in, and a motor began to turn, revealing a stash spot; I gawked at the sight.

"That's for you. Your old man wants you to have it."

It had to be at least 10 bricks in the stash spot . . .

"What is it?" I asked.

"It's coke, 12 kilos to be exact. This shit been sitting for 10 years, I don't know if it loses potency, so be careful with it, ya feel?"

"Pop, yo shit, then unc's," I said with a smile.

"Oh, before I forget, it's bulletproof also," he said.

Vrm, vrm, vrm, my phone buzzed. It was Cowboy. I wasn't about to answer, but something made me pick up. Bang was talking frantically in circles, I could barely make out what he was saying other than . . .

"Cowboy was shot," Bang said.

"What hospital?" I replied, mystified.

"Rockford Memorial," he stated and ended the call.

I looked at Kamar, "Unc, I got to slide. Want me to take the car now?" I said.

"Go see about ya dawg. The car is yours. Call me when you get up with my nigga tomorrow," he said. I slid into the Magnum and grabbed Telay to race to the hospital, the bricks still in the stash spot.

20 minutes later...

Bang, Telay, Nylon, and I sat in the lobby at the hospital.

"What happened?" I asked, looking Bang dead in his eye.

"Mick, fam, he caught us in the hallway. The nigga asked for you, so you might want to stay away from Waaco," he said.

"We all gon' stay away. Kamar hit us with some bricks, so we officially in the game now. Next thing we gon' do is get at these niggas, 'cause it's obvious they were hip to what was going on," I proclaimed.

"Nawl, fuck that! We gon' handle this shit right now. That nigga got Cowboy layin' in this pussy-ass ICU," Bang said, full of rage.

"Yeah, we gotta let these pipes speak," Telay said.

Savon walked up as we plotted our next move, tears streaming down her face. I couldn't help but feel for her seeing her like that. Tiffany came runnin' in asking what had happened.

"One of them bitch-ass niggas shot my brother," Savon said harshly.

The anger she was expressing at the moment had me geeked up.

"How is he doing?" I asked.

Savon sniffled before answering. "He's in a coma," she replied between sobs.

I shook my head. "Come on, y'all, let's go handle this," I said as we exited the hospital.

Back in the basement...

"It's up and stuck at this point," Bang said, holding the H/K with a pair of rabbit ears.

"Them clown-ass niggas should be out right now," I said, then looked to Nylon. "You wit' us, my boi?"

He nodded. "Good, you slide with Bang, as we go lookin' for these bitch-ass niggas," I said.

"They be hangin' out at that liquor store too," Telay proclaimed.

"Don't trip, we gon' find them."

Everybody grabbed a gun and vest and hit the streets in search of our targets. Telay drove as I had the M1 in my lap. My mind was racing with thoughts of how Mick knew we were coming for them. Bang said he asked for me and just got to squeezing. This is what I wanted, but my goal was knocking Flex out the way. If you kill the head, the body will die. However, the animosity I had for Flex ran deeper than me wanting what he had. Flex had killed my mother. I could remember the night he crept into the house. I never said anything about it on the strength that he and my dad were friends. Flex, Kamar, and Calico were thick as thieves until the game changed when my dad got life and they stayed free.

We drove through the city like Call of Duty. I turned to Telay and broke the silence.

"Kamar hit me with 10 bricks of soft, fam. We 'bout to put our foot down out here," I said with sincerity.

"I'm loving all this shit, but what made you want to take over Waaco? I'm gon' ride or die all the way with you, but why now, and why out the blue like this?" Telay asked seriously.

"I'm tired of being a nigga's doormat. We can run this city, fam. It's out there, and we just gotta take it."

"No doubt, but it's enough. Why you driving so hard on Waaco, fam?" he pried.

I couldn't tell Telay I was driven by my own selfish vengeance, and now Cowboy laid in the ICU. "It's 3 in the morning, fam. I think we should finish this mission later today," Telay said.

I agreed with him. "It's late, and we all need some rest for the night. Let's pick up in the A.M."

Same day—SHAREEF'S DINER...

The front bell to the diner chimed as I stepped in. I looked around and then back down to the paper Kamar had given me . . . "Kamar," I mumbled, confirming the name he'd given me.

A waitress walked up with a menu. The place was crowded with patrons.

"Today's special is ranch chicken wings," the young lady said.

I looked her up and down; shorty was light-skinned and beautiful, mesmerizingly so. I cleared my throat nervously, then spoke . . . "Um, is Shareef around?" I asked.

"Yes, I'll get him. You can sit at the bar for now," she said with a chipper and friendly attitude.

The vibe I got from the restaurant was excellent. I would come here to eat anytime, and it was hard to believe it was owned by a dope dealer. Not to mention, the place was literally right next to the police station, so most of the police took their lunch break here. Shareef's able to do it right under their nose, so he must have had a bulletproof game in motion. I sat waiting and scanning the menu. The food looked appetizing, but I wasn't here to eat, I was here on business.

A moment later, a man showed up wearing a kufi, rocking a thick beard that was well-trimmed and lined up, sorta like Rick Ross. He wore designer garments like the ones French Montana used to wear.

"As-salamu alaykum," he greeted as he approached me.

I looked at him up and down awkwardly. Shareef's appearance had thrown me for a loop; he was Arabic with dark skin, but his accent was Mid-Eastern. We shook hands.

"Kamar sent me down, he said that you could prolly help me with . . . umm . . . um," I stuttered.

He chuckled. "I know what you here for, Ock, so don't let my look fool you. I am Muslim, but I'm a hustler too, Ocky," he said, then smiled. Shareef looked to be deeply religious, with a special exception for the American dream.

"How much weight can you move?" Shareef asked me, breaking the ice.

I thought for a minute, then realized I didn't have clientele, or even a shake spot. I was green to the game, and if I told him the truth, my career could end here and now.

"Long as the product's good, I could do whatever money will buy," I said.

"Okay, Ock, let me rephrase the question: what you want to spend?" he altered the question.

"What's the ticket on a few ounces?" I asked.

He laughed. "You can't be serious, Ock. K sent you, so I'ma put 10 thousand of these blues on you and 2 kilos of raw heroin. This the purest dope in the city, it's all pure Afghan, Ock. I want 60 per kilo and 50 cents for the blues. You do good with that, and I'll stretch you out further. You think you can handle that?" he asked.

"Whatever you throw my way, I'm gon' make disappear," I replied.

"Alright, Ock, you got what you need, and I got some other shit to handle. My waitress gon' get you a to-go, she'll meet you at the door."

We shook hands, and I exited back outside to the Magnum. I put the bricks in the stash spot, then drove to Telay's house. He was in his room playing his PS5, so I barged in unannounced and threw the dope on the bed.

"It's time to get busy," I said, looking him in the eye.

"How we supposed to sell all this shit?" Telay asked.

"Rene, she used to buy dope off my dad back in the day. She out south, but we can pull up on her, and she'll help."

I opened the key of heroin, then broke 2 oz's off the brick, while Telay helped count 500 blues.

"We taking this with us. Stash the rest," I said, and we were out the door.

Rene's house SOUTHSIDE...

Telay and I stood on Rene's porch, waiting for someone to answer the door. I knocked again. We could hear motion from inside the house when the door swung open, and Rene squinted . . . "Zaro, is that you?" she said, opening her arms wide for a hug.

Rene was the come-to junkie for everything; she was the link to all the other j's. She knew where all the best dope in town was and had helped Flex pump Waaco upside. She even brought most of their clientele. Rene could shake a nuke, as the junkies called it.

"It's me, aunty," I replied as we embraced.

She looked at Telay, then back to me.

"What brings you to the southside?" she said.

"I need your help."

"What you need, honey?"

"You. Trying to make some money?" I asked.

"Sure, come on in," she said as she opened the door for us.

As Telay and I cruised through her house, we brushed past tons of junkies, wall to wall. I looked around cautiously as she led the way to the kitchen. I turned the backpack upside down on the table, and as the drugs littered the tabletop, Rene looked greedily.

"I need you to whip me up a Tesla," I asked.

She examined the drugs thoroughly, then went to work . . .

(BANG)

Cornoe's Liquor Store, near WAACO...

"That's the Range Rover they be ridin' in," I said, sitting low in my seat.

"What now? You want to pop off right here?" Nylon asked.

"Nawl, let's follow them out of here and catch 'em by surprise. They don't know what we ridin' in. We can take 'em by surprise."

I watched as Mick came out the store holding a bottle, then waited as he talked to a female. As he went back to the

Range Rover, I bit my bottom lip angrily and shook my head while gripping my F/N. I was ready to put a hole in Mick. They rode down West State Street unaware they were being tailed.

"When we get to the stoplight, I'm gonna pull up to the side of his car and you let it ride, fam," I said.

Nylon had the look of a monster in his eye. He slid the slide on the mini Drako with the Mickey Mouse drum attached. I rolled the window down as we stopped at a light.

Fa! Fa! Fa! Fa! Fa! Fa!

As he swept the side of the car, Mick's brains splattered the front window, and Calico mashed the gas pedal, running the light. I gave chase; as Calico did a U-turn a block down, his arm came out the window as his Mac-90 jumped around in his hand.

Boc! Boc! Boc! Boc!

The windshield cracked, glass shattered all over the back seat of the Range Rover. As he drove recklessly back up West State Street towards Waaco, I called Zaro to let him know what happened.

(O'RILEY)

One week later...

As Marty and I drove to the meet spot, O'Mally set coalition with the IRA and the bikers. It would be held at the convention center within the Howard Johnson Motel. Marty sat in the passenger seat, something bothering him, and I hadn't seen him like that in a long time. The car was dead silent, so I broke the silence.

"What's on your mind, mate?" I asked.

"O'Mally. That mutha-fuka's crazy! You ever noticed the way he looks at me? Sometimes I think he knows we're informants and is just waiting on the opportunity to strike," he remarked nervously.

I had to laugh at his candor.

"You're just being paranoid, lad. If O'Mally suspected anything, we'd already be dead."

I parked, the place looking like a biker convention with all the cycles parked everywhere. Bruiser came rolling in on a chopper as we walked to the door. Once inside, Marty tapped me on the shoulder . . .

"Who's the biker over there with the black vest on? Isn't—isn't that the guy I had to go to court on 15 years ago? He works for that crew out of Chicago, the Dirty Whiteboys," he said.

"If it is, then what's he doing here? Bikers and Dirty Whiteboys been at each other's throats for years now, they despise each other," I stated.

"What if he makes me for an informant?"

"He won't do that. He'll be afraid you'll make him for a traitor to his organization."

Everyone entered into the conference room of the motel, bikers seated on one side and IRA on the other. O'Mally sat at the head of the table, and Bruiser walked in late, with the Dirty Whiteboy in tow. Marty squirmed nervously in his seat and kept his gaze in the man's direction . . .

"You see that?" Marty remarked, sounding like a scared toddler.

"Pipe down, lad, you're overreacting. That might not even be him," I replied.

Marty and I were a dynamic duo as informants come, but sometimes we worked separately. This Dirty Whiteboy was one of those times, but Marty got him a life sentence, so there was no way it could possibly be him. I thought Marty was seeing ghosts. As O'Mally began to address the room, all the chatter ceased quickly. O'Mally was built like a UFC fighter, his hair orange like the Fighting Irish, and he bore a scar underneath his cheek, as if someone tried to cut his face off. This gave his look a venomous aura, and with soul-piercing, narrow eyes to top it off, it seemed like he could see right through you. He began to speak...

"We're here today to discuss a possible merge with the IRA and Devil's Angels. Bruiser and his adviser Steve are here speaking on behalf of those bikers today, am I right?" he said, then looked to Bruiser for a response.

Bruiser stood up and in a raspy tone replied, "You got that, bud."

"This meth you guys are getting, what's its purity level? I mean, we got an idea, but I want to know what it is before you guys start attacking it," O'Mally started right to business.

"It's 100 percent pure as the driven sun, we haul straight from Mexico ourselves twice a month. All we need is a distributor to help back our portion."

"What do you mean by portion? I thought you guys had full control of your shipments?" O'Mally asked.

"We have the 1st of the month, but the second goes to the cartel. Our pay is just for the 1st shipment," he replied.

I leaned over and whispered in Marty's ear, "These cocksuckers are as dumb as they look."

Bruiser and his crew were getting paid in drugs; they were taking double the risk. This would be the perfect time for us to swoop in and take a portion of their pie with minimal risk.

"My guys can help you distribute your portion, but what is the take?" O'Mally asked.

"About 400 pounds, give or take," he said.

"That's good, what else?" O'Mally inquired.

"My guys and I want part of the *Lucky 7* pub, our men like to gamble. We can bring a lot of business," Bruiser said.

I jumped up angrily . . . "The pub's off-limits, we'll move the product ourselves. You guys can keep your own territory and collect," I exclaimed.

Bruiser leaned back and rubbed his beard in defeat. I stared over at him like an angered pit bull. My territory was marked, and I wouldn't budge. The bikers brought a lot of damage and brawlers with them, and a lot of people disliked them 'cause of the destruction they caused.

71

"I'm sure we can come to terms some sort of way," O'Mally said.

That's when Steve offered his words; he stood and spoke
. . .

"I'm sure we can come to some sort of agreement."

"We'll give you guys a portion of the product on the southside for 20 percent of your gambling profits at the Lucky 7 since you guys don't wanna come off of the bar," Bruiser interjected.

"Okay, it's set then, let's get outta here before the cops show up," O'Mally said jokingly.

O'Mally closed the meeting, and everyone filed out of the convention center. As we all exited through the front lobby, O'Mally hung back. I noticed Steve and Bruiser talking to him, but I paid them no attention as we exited the building. *Vrm! Vrm! Vrm!* My phone vibrated, the caller ID read Roger
. . .

"The fuck does this cunt want?" I muttered.

We talked for a moment, and I agreed to let him meet me at the bar.

(ROGER)

One hour later—THE LUCKY 7...

I bundled my jacket and stuck my face into it as I walked towards the bar, shivering from the cold and the fear of talking to O'Riley, 'cause I owed him a lot of money that I just didn't have. I was forced to stay back from work after the robbery, and the police were all over me like I was a co-defendant in the heist. I helped out, but the only thing I got was hardship on my family. Amy was so shaken up from the fact that one of the guys had almost killed her. He'd fired his gun next to her, but it was a close brush with death, and she'd felt his want to kill her but that he just couldn't muster the courage to pull the trigger.

I stepped into the pub and noticed the place was lively with patrons and gamblers; its atmosphere came with a lot of bad memories though. I'd gotten low on my pills, and I needed a fix, being the reason I showed up, but I hadn't paid O'Riley any of what I owed him. I was going out on a limb by showing up at all, but the robbery had put so much stress on me that I needed some relief.

I was stopped by one of the bouncers named John. He was a muscular, hardcore type.

"What you doin' here? This place for paying customers," he said aggressively.

"Can you tell O'Riley I'm here?" I said, trying to look around the guy.

At that moment though, he came walking in with Marty in tow. I hoped I could get through to him, as I was going through withdrawals.

"Hey, O'Riley!" I shouted as I saw him enter from what had to be a side entrance.

As he turned in my direction, I stepped his way, but John put his hand on my chest, stopping me. O'Riley began walking my way . . .

"What's he doing here?" O'Riley stated.

"I need another loan. I got a lawsuit that I'm about to get, and it should be here any day. I'll have you all the way paid off by then," I proclaimed.

"I've heard that sad story before. I want my fuckin' money. You got one week, and I'm sending the dog after that. Now get the hell outta here."

"Please—please don't do me this way," I pleaded.

"Take him out back and tell him what I said." O'Riley finished.

John spun me around then hauled me out back roughly . . .

"Wait a minute," I begged.

He continued to drag me out until we were in the back alley. I got hit and beat with closed fists and baseball bats, but after a short period, John got tired of kicking me in the rear and let me go walk to my car. I never felt like less of a man.

I looked in my rearview mirror—my eyes black and lips fat; John had worked a number on me. I drove home in excruciating pain, and as I got closer to the Gold Star Hotel, I thought about what I would have to spin to my wife, Amy. The next thought I had was where I could score some heroin. I had a friend on the south side who had a shooting gallery where people could get high. Rene could surely help me in my time of need.

(ZARO)

Rene's house trap of the year....

The front and back door at Rene's were in perpetual use. The heroin I'd gotten from Shareef was A1, but the blues were even better. Customers were pouring in, and we started working the spot in shifts. As Nylon and I sat in the kitchen counting money, Rene worked the outside, bringing the customers in. She promoted the reaper, and we had numerous overdoses from its potency. Nylon looked at me with a fist full of bills . . .

"No cap, fam, this bitch rockin'. I ain't never seen this much money in one spot before. This might be goin' harder than Waaco," Nylon said.

"Waaco still my target, I don't give a fuck how much we make over here. We get Waaco, we gon' be unstoppable," I said.

"Bang and I let them niggas have it the other night," Nylon said vehemently.

"I like that. Now we gotta put Flex and Calico down. Them niggas comin' gang."

"I put that boy's brains in Calico's lap, so they know shit ain't sweet," he bragged.

Nylon killed Mick, but that was only the beginning. Calico would take the city to war over Mick, so we all had to keep our distance from Waaco. The southside was our home, for now. Cowboy was left in a coma though, which made this a lot worse than it appeared on the surface. A knock came at the door.

"It's your turn," Nylon said, as he separated the bills in his hands.

I rose from my seat, but Rene beat me to the door.

"Don't worry about it, I got you. Y'all can pay me to get the door too!" Rene said, as she wobbled to the door with her big south country backside. I went back to the kitchen with Nylon.

"I bet Rene got some good dope-fiend pussy," Nylon remarked.

I stared at him with my nose turned up . . .

"Boy, stop, you ain't never hit no smoker late night? I can't wait till it ain't got no money," Nylon joked, half serious.

"Yo' dick gon' fall off," I replied.

Rene stepped into the kitchen, and my heart almost stopped when I saw who was behind her.

"I need a 10 pack for my old friend Roger," Rene said, and handed me 10 twenty-dollar bills.

I paused nervously at the sight. I wasn't sure if Roger had made me, but the way it appeared, he was more concerned with getting high.

"Rene, you mind if I use the basement?" Roger asked.

"By all means, long as you got some for Rene," she spoke of herself in the 3rd person.

I tried to say as little as possible in case he recognized my voice.

Rene and Roger ducked off to the shooting spot in the basement, and Nylon looked over at me, confused.

"What was that about, my boi?" he said.

"Your guess is better than mine, gang. I'm lost along with you."

"That's what he had those pills for. He was using them shits," Nylon stated, then went back to sifting through bills.

"He prolly just usin' the dope to cope with his wife's death."

"Man, that bitch ain't dead, I've been scanning the news networks, and I don't think Cowboy had the stomach to do that shit," Nylon proclaimed.

"I figured as much. You know we had to let Cowboy stunt on us so he could feel better, right?" I laughed, missing Cowboy's narcissistic ways . . .

Vrm! Vrm! Vrm! My phone vibrated, and I looked at the tag. It was Savon. I answered, talked briefly, then ended the call. She had been camped out at the hospital and wanted me to bring her some food. I agreed, leaving Nylon at Rene's by himself. He had his Drako and a F/N, so I knew he could handle himself if anything came up. Cowboy was still in the ICU in a coma and had been for almost a week now. All of us had been so busy with the streets that no one had offered Savon any comfort as a friend. Telay and Bang were out running the city rugged, with Bang devoting his time to tracking Flex's whereabouts, and Telay putting his time to use hustling the blues up in Beloit, Wisconsin. I slipped into the Magnum and drove to Rockford Memorial. Savon sat at her brother's bedside with her hair mangled, though still with that sexy vibe about her I found infatuating. She looked up at me as I walked in.

"Hey, Zaro, I'm glad you came. I've been here for days, and the hospital food is starting to taste bland," she said.

"This my nigga right here, I can't leave him or you on stuck," I said.

We embraced each other tightly, then I heard the toilet flush suddenly, and Tiffany stepped out.

"What's up, youngin'?" she greeted.

We pulled apart cordially.

"Sup, Tif," I replied.

She looked me up and down, noticing my Amiri jeans and Gucci sneakers...

DRILL CITY | ZAY'TOWVEN

"Okay, look at you. Somebody came up out here," Tif said with a sensual smirk.

I wasn't the one to show out, though I did cop some new clothes. Tif is a greedy bitch and wasn't my type at all. My crush was on the same girl it's always been for years now, but with my friendship with Cowboy, I didn't dare. Tif was Telay's speed; he liked them raunchy, while Savon, on the other hand, was a Diva; beauty with smarts. Telay would love for her to acknowledge him the way she was with me; I'm sure if she'd see him saucey though, her attention would be on him the same exact way.

"The doctor said he could be like this for a long time, but that they could take him off the machine anytime. I don't have the money to pay for the ventilator," Savon said painfully. I could tell her heart was hurting immensely.

"How much is the tab for the vent?" I asked.

"I'm not for certain, but I'm sure it's not cheap."

The beeps and quietness signified how serious the situation was as I looked at Cowboy lying motionless on that gurney. I had to do something to save him, I couldn't just let the doctors pull the plug on him . . . not like that.

"Where do you want to eat at?" I asked.

"I'd prefer if you would pick something up for me."

"I want something too," Tif interjected.

I looked at her in disgust, she was always in the middle of something she had no business in.

"A'ight, what y'all want?" I asked.

While Savon and Tif decided what they wanted, a doctor entered the room. I inquired about Cowboy's situation by asking the price of leaving him on the ventilator.

"Upwards of 200,000," he said.

I was taken aback by the cost. That was a lot of money for any of us to produce. I did have it to spend, however, and I knew just how to get it to him safely.

"How long does he have to be on here before he'll have to spend the money?" I asked.

"Three days, so I suggest you get his affairs in order and make the proper accommodations. He doesn't have insurance, so we can't keep him here much longer," Doctor Ramsey said.

I exhaled deeply in frustration. The doctor left as smoothly as he came, and I looked to Savon, who had started sobbing again, and hugged her...

"It's gonna be okay," I promised, and meant every word.

Chapter 8

(FLEX)

Days later in WAACO...

My crew stood in the confines of a small apartment along with Remo and his crew. The dining room table was cluttered with pipes; Mick had been murdered, and in light of the recent beef, we were also losing profits. I glared around the room, everyone acutely aware that I was hotter than fish grease right now . . . except Remo. Remo looked around as if shit was cool though; I took it as a sort of betrayal and told myself I couldn't trust him any further than I could throw him. I drew my gaze his way . . .

"Fuck is goin' on?" I asked Remo.

"What you mean? I'm doing the best I can, fam. This shit's not my fault," he answered.

I paced back and forth, the bricks I'd gotten from Shareef had stagnated our motion. We'd slowed dramatically, and there was only one thing that could've caused the problem—Remo's grimy ass. He's prolly cutting the dope too hard and putting the good shit somewhere else. I hoped he wasn't that stupid though because his chef game was impeccable, which put accidents out of the question. To me, he was a snake-ass nigga though. Puerto Ricans were a slimy lot, so it could be why our sales had dropped dramatically.

"My guys ain't doin' nothin' different with the cut . . . I don't know why shit slowed up. Maybe 'cause them lil' young niggas you got runnin' round here playing Call of

Duty got niggas scared to come into Waaco now. You already got Mick killed behind this nonsense."

I thought for a moment as I let his words resonate with me. He'd made a good point, as they were posted up around the projects shooting at potential customers. Waaco's D-line was the best in the city though, niggas would die for the dope, and Remo had niggas dying off his blend all the time. Now they were shopping elsewhere? My paranoia made me think that Remo had some side shit goin' on.

The look on his face had my blood boiling. He was taking this shit way too lightly. On impulse, I jumped up and rushed him. I stuck him in his jaw, and he stumbled backwards.

"You think I'm stupid, nigga?" I huffed, out of breath from swinging on him wildly.

I stepped back, allowing him the opportunity to recover from my assault, my chest heaving as everyone looked at me like I was mad. Niggas stood with their arms crossed watching.

Calico sat back laughing at the whole situation while my anger got the best of me. Remo tried to fight back a little, but I humiliated him in front of our guys. My shoulders spoke for me, and they articulated clearly. Calico finally decided to defuse the situation.

"Big dawg, ya boy might be right. Much as I hate to agree with the nigga, as I would love nothin' more than for you to beat him to death. The shorty who Mick shot up's friends are still out there makin' shit hot for us. On top of that, they upped the ante by killing Mick," Calico said.

"My nigga, I'm aware of that, but they fuckin' with my money now," I cursed.

Remo stood, dabbing the blood from his lip, and as I looked over at him, he looked like a straight goofy.

"What we gon' do about this situation?" Remo asked.

"Start by you stop acting like a lame and get to this money. Put yo' guys in the street and find out where all the j's goin'. Calico, get the wolf-pack ready, and y'all tear the streets up 'til them niggas is dead," I said.

We all dispersed from the apartment except for Remo; Calico looked at him and shook his head as he headed out the door.

"Aye, let me holla at you," I asked.

Remo spun in his tracks to face me, an altercation in the making. This wasn't the first time we'd gone through something of this nature, and I knew in the end I'd end up apologizing to him. We were a team and we needed each other, but I still felt like he'd stole from me and then disrespected Mick. Mick was my dawg, and for Remo to use his name in vain . . . well, it would not be tolerated, to say the least.

"What's up, fam?" he said tiredly, like I was bothering him.

This nigga was acting like a lil' bitch. That's why I hit him the first time, so I forced myself to swallow my pride and calm down.

"Let me talk to you, my boy," I said.

"Fam, what we got to speak about? It's all business, nothin' more," he replied.

"Let it be that then, just make sure them numbers are right."

"This my last re-up with you, Flex. Me and my niggas 'bout to go our own way. I ain't gon' leave you on stuck though, I'll show you our whip game, then we out," he said.

I didn't reply, just nodded. I knew this day was coming.

"Okay, my nigga, I wanna apologize. I know we've had our differences, but I don't want us to separate like this, fam. It was only business. I'm stressing and ain't seeing clear right now," I said.

He looked at me with pleading eyes. We embraced, and I knew the nigga was soft as butter. I laughed to myself as we hugged, knowing my plan was to cross him and that we were coming to a fork in the road.

"I got an idea if you double the load. I know how to get all our customers back, and I got some niggas in Indiana that will cop some weight off us," he said.

I shook my head, thinking about Mikey and his bitch we had to put to sleep last week.

Remo chuckled, "I know what you thinking, and I ain't talkin' 'bout none of Mikey's people."

"What you talkin'?"

"3500 an oz all the way out."

I rubbed my palms together; the offer sounded tasty, and that kinda deal would make up for the losses we've been incurring. I curled my lip and nodded...

"Imma hit Shareef and get the weight, how much you got?" I asked.

"My money is tied up in something at the moment, but I'm sure to get it back on a quick flip."

This was my time to get over. "I want a 70/30 split on this run since I got to put up all the money."

He exhaled deeply; it was evident I had got him by the balls.

"Come on, Flex, don't be that way," he pleaded.

"Fam, this is business, I'm taking a big risk here with you talkin' about leaving."

"What if I stick around for a minute? Imma be honest, my bitch hit my stash and she took me for 200,000. My dick is in the dirt right now, so please do sixty-forty for me one time and let me bounce back," he said.

I paused like it was actually something to think about, then said what I had planned the whole while: "Sixty-five," I stated greedily.

Remo exhaled deeply. I could tell the frustration had got to him. I looked him in the eye while he folded like a lawn chair.

"You got a deal," he replied.

We shook hands, then hit the streets.

I met Shareef at the diner, and he agreed to give me the extra weight, so I spent my last hundred bands on some kilos of raw dope. I dropped the pack off in Waaco, and Calico and I got back in traffic to head to West State Street. I kept my sight trained on the rearview mirror to make sure I wasn't being tailed.

"Twelve is behind us . . . don't do nothin' stupid," I said.

Calico took his pipe off his hip, then put it in the passenger-side stash spot. The police always pulled us over looking for guns whenever we left Waaco. It had become a normal occurrence, but these weren't normal police; they were gang unit and were more aggressive than other policemen. I braced myself for what was to come; usually, we knew whenever raids would come because the narcs would send informants, so this was their only surprise tactic—a traffic stop. They never found anything, however, as we had stash spots all over every car. We drove almost a block before their lights flickered.

"They on us, fam. I'm 'bout to pull over," I said nervously.

"It's Officer Tully," I stated as he stepped out of the unmarked patrol car.

Tully was a *Robocop* dickhead who worked for the gang unit. Both car doors opened, and they drew their weapons while Tully ordered us out the car. I shook my head as they went through the motions as if we had robbed a bank; they cuffed us as we exited the vehicle, then Tully spun me around.

"Look at me, asshole. You know what's goin' on here?" he said.

Tully was so far in my face I could smell the salami sandwich and coffee on his breath.

"Look around at my new friends. You recognize these guys?" he said.

I scanned all the crew-cut white boys, noticing they looked as if Vanilla Ice had collaborated with Marky Mark and the Funky Bunch. I shook my head at his question.

"This is a new gang unit with the FBI. We cover all the surrounding areas and focus on nothing but gang activity . . . *and* shootings!" he said.

"That shit's got nothin' to do with me, fuck is you on us for?" I replied.

"When's the last time you been to Indiana?"

I chuckled. "I hate Indiana. I'm more of a Cali type of guy," I said humorously.

"Funny, eh?" he said, then put Calico and me in the back of the unmarked.

He stuck his head inside, grunted, then said: "Let's see how bad you are when we take you down for murder, asshole," he hissed and slammed the door. I knew they didn't have shit on us, as the only witness they could've had was Mick, and he was dead. Calico and I had been in this same spot before; you don't say shit, they don't know shit . . .

(ROGER)

Gold Star Motel...

My addiction had gotten worse. I was spending more and more time at Rene's house getting high, and now Amy and I got into a big feud, and she left to her mother's house. I was all alone as I sat and watched old cowboy flicks; the urge to use had overtaken me. *Vrm! Vrm! Vrm!* My phone buzzed. It was O'Riley. He'd given me a week to come up with his money after roughing me up in the alley behind the *Lucky 7* pub. I'd had a really bad few weeks between the bank getting robbed and the two cops breathing down my neck. I didn't know what to do anymore. My phone vibrated for a second time; this time it was Amy, though. I hurriedly answered.

"Roger, we need you," she said between sobs.

"What's the matter? Where are you?" I asked.

"I'm at the police station, they want you to come down."

"What? How? How? I don't understand," I replied.

"They linked my car to the robbery somehow. I was scared and had to tell them everything."

"Shit," I muttered. "I'm on my way there now." I had to go save my wife.

I ended the call and went to the restroom to wash my face. When I looked in the mirror, I looked awful. I hadn't shaved in days because my life was in shambles. I heard a car pull up, then the door slam shut, so I walked to the door to see an old Lincoln Town Car parked out front. No one was there, so I went back to the restroom and brushed my teeth when a light tap came on the door.

"Who is it?" I asked as I moved closer to the door, holding my breath.

"Room service," a female voice said from the other side of the door.

I dried my hair and opened the door to see a nice lil' redhead chick standing before me with a handful of blankets. Suddenly, the fabric from the blankets flew towards me, and I backed up to see the woman holding a small pistol with a lion's snout. My eyes immediately bulged. The pistol was muffled . . . *Pew! Pew! Pew!* I fell to the floor, my breathing erratic as I coughed and choked on my own blood. I stared into the woman's eyes as she stood over me; she pointed the barrel at me, so I was looking down it. Despite her slicer, the woman's beauty was tantalizing.

"Luck of the Fighting Irish," she said, then the gun continued spewing into my chest, *Pew! Pew! Pew!*

My entire life flashed before my eyes, my sight darkened, and, while still choking on my own blood, death became me as I drifted away.

(ZARO)

SLIDING THE CITY...

Lil Zoo hopped into the Magnum with me, an ounce of crack lay in my lap.

"What I gotta do to get on y'all level?" he asked.

I chuckled at his remark; it was a fact that we were at the top of our game, but there were still problems I had. Namely, getting rid of this nigga Flex. Mick was dead, but my target was the big dawg. I wanted Waaco for me and my niggas; we were hungry and ready to take the throne. Zoo was from California, and he ain't have no loyalties or dedication to anybody over here. We met a while back when I sold nickel bags of reggie, he was a young dread head then, and we called him Zoo because in school he used to smell like an animal. Everyone made fun of him except me; I embraced him as a friend because his family was like mine—broken. He was out of his element and had no one to count on but himself.

He was the type of guy you didn't want to trust, as he was a wolf; I learned to keep the wolves close though, and let the snakes lie in the grasses. I needed niggas like him on my team if I'm going up against Waaco. Doing it all by ourselves would be a hard, if not impossible, task. I looked Zoo up and down; his shoes were worn, his clothes were dingy, and his dreads were frizzy. His skin looked like he'd been outside for days, and when I saw him walking on the way to the corner store, I took it as fate. This was a perfect opportunity to recruit an extra, so I told him to hop in, and we started spinning blocks. I originally had in mind to give him the whole zip, but then I had a better idea.

"I got a trap on the east side if you tryna work it?" I asked.

"Gang, my dick is in the dirt right now, and I'll do anything to get some paper. My mom is sick, and we ain't got shit," he replied.

I had opened a new spot on the east side of town. Telay ran it, selling crack and powder keys that Kamar had given me. We had the block house on the southside and a rock spot on the east, so our crew was split up. Telay and Bang ran the rocks, with Nylon and I pushing the d-line. We had it going crazy, with the spot doing ten thousand a day. I figured I could let him relieve Nylon's shift for a while, and I could watch him myself...

"I'm ready for whatever, gang. When do I start?" he said anxiously.

I drove towards Rene's house to see a line from the front door extending nearly down the whole block. I looked on in amazement but knew if it continued to be this obvious, the cops would be on us in no time. I had to figure something else out. I looked to Zoo and got the perfect idea to put him on perimeter control so the traffic would be organized and efficient. He looked at the d-line in complete awe.

He turned to me and said, "This yo' shit, gang?"

"It's ours. Me and my niggas running this," I said as we both slid out the Magnum.

He nodded, astonished at what he was seeing. We pushed our way through the crowd of people, and I used the back door to avoid the line. I should've directed the traffic around the backyard, as there was an alleyway entrance that would help divert attention off the front street. I was always thinking of ways to upgrade our operation.

Nylon was passing out blows as I walked in, piles of money littering the table. I went into the kitchen and handed Zoo a Beretta 9 milli.

"This you, fam. We gotta protect the spot," I said.

He stuffed the gun in his waist as Nylon finished up on the midday rush. He looked at Zoo...

"What you doing here?" he asked.

"Tryna get some money, gang," he answered, then looked at all the money on the table.

"I need you to control traffic outside, so just walk around the block and call if you see anything outta the ordinary. For now, you can stay inside with us and help count this paper," I said.

He nodded his head, then began taking off his jacket. He took the gun I'd given him off his waistline and took a seat, setting it in his lap. He picked up a wad of twenties, and Nylon glared at me strangely. I smirked and nodded; I knew what he was thinking.

Hours later...
I woke up from my nap. Nylon was on the other couch still asleep and Rene was nowhere in sight. I scanned the room then walked to the kitchen. Where the fuck this nigga Zoo at? I thought.

(FLEX)

WAACO stash house...
The feds held Calico and me for the max time, 3 days, on some murder questioning shit. We pulled up to Waaco, and I peeped the lines of customers wasn't out like usual. I had a fresh re-up in the buildings before the feds grabbed us, so what the fuck was goin' on . . .

"Somethin' ain't right 'bout this shit, big dawg," Calico said.

"I know," I replied.

"I gotta talk to Remo. This shit crazy," I said, hopin' he ain't step on the dope too hard and ran all the customers off. I walked into the stash house and saw one of my workers posted up on the couch playin' Madden. I looked at him like he was dirt.

"What the fuck goin' on in here?" I said, pissed at what I was seeing.

He looked up at me, surprised.

"Damn, I'm glad to see you two niggas. They said the feds picked yawl up."

"They did, but fuck all that. That ain't what's important right now. Why the fuck this shit look so slow?" I asked.

"Remo pulled all his people out the shake houses when you hit him. They dipped in the middle of the night with everything."

I shook my head. "FUCK, FUCK, FUCK! Y'all stupid ass niggas ain't try to stop him? I can't believe this shit," I shouted, full of rage.

"He said the feds was gonna be here next, and we ain't know what to do. He got ownership in this too, so we been takin' orders from him."

"You can't be serious. How y'all let this nigga rob us?" I yelled.

"You had most of us scoping out who was fuckin' with our money. It's some niggas on the southside, Zaro Neem, they been makin' noise 'round here, and they been busin' them pipes," he said.

"I want y'all to shut that shit down tonight. I wanna hear on the news, '*A thousand rounds went off and everybody dead.*' Don't come back 'til it's done," I ordered.

Calico smirked, "I can't wait to smoke one of them niggas," he said, hyped up.

"Nawl, gang, I need you with me. We gotta find this nigga Remo, and his BM stay on the east side, so I think he hidin' over there," I replied.

(REMO)

REMO'S baby mom's house...

"Sit back and enjoy, daddy," Kee Kee said in a seductive tone, as she pushed me back onto the love seat. "I'm 'bout to drain your body of every drop of cum you have in it."

She started grinding all over me and twisting her body like a snake. Before long, she had stripped away all her clothing articles as Jaques played loudly throughout the house. She massaged her DD's in my face, looking me seductively in the eyes. She snaked her long tongue around her nipple, and with her right hand, she played with her dripping pussy. My dick was hard inside my Ethika underwear. She pulled her fingers from her womb, then put her index finger to her tongue and licked her juices. I could smell the sweetness of her pussy, and it drove my hormones wild. I felt like an animal in the wild. She rose from my lap and stood on the hinds of her legs while looking at me with those hazel-brown eyes. She bent over and tugged at my underwear before ending up on her knees in front of me. She fished for my pole, and in one smooth movement, she'd retrieved her prize. She looked at it seductively, trying to figure out where to start. She spit on it and started to stroke the shaft slowly. She licked the tip and wrapped her tongue around the head; after a few seconds of playing with her food, she devoured me, slowly plunging her face into my abdomen. She kept going until there was nothing left to see of my manhood. Her head bobbed back and forth while she made succulent slurping sounds . . .

"Uhm!" I grunted with pleasure.

I enjoyed the wetness of her mouth for at least 20 minutes. She let her breasts rest in my lap and rubbed my dick on her face as if it were a marker. My shit was harder than Chinese algebra as she looked downwards and let a gob of spit go on her breast; she put my dick between them and slowly started to let me fuck her tits. I tilted my head backward, the pleasure I was feeling was off the scale as my dick slid between her massive mammaries. Occasionally she would reload spit on them to keep them slippery, and just as I was about to drop my load, she pulled back and stood up to straddle me.

I had to see what that pussy felt like. My dick-head throbbed as it slid inside her, smooth and easy, her pussy wetter than a slip 'n' slide, clinging to me with every inch. The heat of her wrapped around me, sending waves of ecstasy through my body. She arched her back, grinding on me, her body moving in rhythm with the music. Her lips brushed against my ear as she nibbled it, sending shivers down my spine. She teased my earlobe with her tongue, slow and deliberate, making me feel like I was being licked by fire. Her movements were relentless, up and down, as she rode me, pulling me deeper, driving me wild with every motion.

Kee Kee was a force—her sex game was why we had three beautiful kids together. The sounds she made were pure seduction, like nothing I'd ever heard before. Every moan, every gasp, went straight to my soul, making me ache for more. I could feel the pressure building, the tingle deep in my scrotum, until I couldn't hold back. My body trembled as I shivered, feeling my release rise from the pit of my stomach. She must've felt it too because, in an instant, she was on me again, her mouth back on my dick, sucking me hard and deep, not stopping until I exploded in her mouth.

She swallowed every drop, licking me clean like it was her favorite treat. My cum clung to her tongue, and she wrapped it around her like a spaghetti strand, savoring every last bit, making sure I stayed hard for her. She never let go, sucking and teasing me until I felt like I was losing control, my body weightless, floating in pure ecstasy, unable to resist the pull of her every move. The way she held me inside her mouth, knowing I was still hard, only drove me further into lust. Each time she pulled back, her mouth just barely leaving me, I was left aching, wanting more. The rhythm of her movements pushed me to the edge. I couldn't help myself—every time she took me deeper, every time her tongue traced my length, it made me crave her even more. We fucked for hours, my hips thrusting deep: I was lost in the pleasure of it all. When she finally collapsed, exhausted and spent, she fell asleep with me still inside her, our bodies tangled together.

We fucked and sucked for hours until she fell asleep.

I got up then unzipped the Amiri tote bag and smiled at the contents that I'd stole from Flex. Ol' dumb-ass brunt of a nigga didn't see the shit coming, I'd been playing him for months waiting on my opportunity to rob him. This was pre-planned, and him getting picked up just made it happen prematurely, but what's done is done, and I was on my way to South Dakota in the morning.

There was no way this nigga could catch me. He hurt my pride, but in the end, I hurt his pockets. I gaped inside the bag, the three kilos of raw heroin inside, and unzipped the other that had 100 bands. 'Twas a good lick, I thought to myself. When I heard the Feds had this dumb-ass nigga for questioning on a body, I made my move. I couldn't believe he was holding out the way he was with me and just shook my head at the thought of him playing with the bulls out here. I chuckled, then picked up my phone. I had an idea that would keep him busy for a while. I dialed the number, and main man picked up on the 3rd ring.

"Who the fuck is this?" he asked in a groggy voice; it was 3 a.m.

"Ya knight in shining armor, nigga, Remo. It was Flex and Calico that put the hit on you," I said.

"What!"

"Yeah, it was Flex who had the youngin' run up on you," I said, then ended the call.

I smiled, hearing the surprise and the anger in his tone. Then I hit the young boy Zaro and gave him some locations on Flex, mainly his spot up in Belvidere. That's why niggas couldn't find him when shit got hot, and he didn't even know I knew that shit. I was always two steps ahead of him. I already had a buy of the dope O'Riley wants, with one of the kilos allocated to him today and one tomorrow. Flex would be too busy getting shot at to catch up with me, and I'd be long gone before he knew it.

(FLEX)

Outside REMO'S baby mamma house...
"What's the plan, big dawg?" Calico asked.

This was strange. There was no car outside this bitch's house other than hers. I thought about it, and it made sense considering he must've been hiding his shit and driving hers anyway. A'ight, I know what Imma do...

"We 'bout to run up in there, kidnap her and the kid, and sell him his family back," I said, then slid the hammer back on my Glock 29. Calico followed my lead as we crept around the house looking for a way in. We peeped through all the windows, and the house was completely dark. Calico and I met back up in the backyard.

"You find a way in?" I asked.

"Hell no," he replied.

We stood in the backyard trying to figure it out, then I said, "We gon' have to kick the door. I noticed the guest room entrance, let's go in through there."

Calico and I found our way in and drew our guns as we skulked about the house, clearing rooms one at a time. My gun was leading the way as I went room to room when I heard light breathing in one of the last rooms. I signaled quietly for Calico to come over and stepped inside the room. It was engulfed in darkness, but even with the bed covers bunched up, you could tell there was someone underneath. I woke whomever it was with the barrel of my gun.

"Ahhhh!" she screamed loudly.

She tried to jump up and move around, but the sheets fought her every step of the way. I snatched her up by her hair and dragged her to her feet.

"Bitch, where that nigga at?!" I demanded.

"I don't know who you talking 'bout," she cried out.

Calico scoured throughout the house before we met up in the living room. He held a small child in his arms.

"I'mma murk this baby if you don't tell me where the fuck your baby daddy is," Calico stated viciously.

"He is in jail," she said.

"Okay, this bitch think I'm playin'."

I tied her up then threw her in the trunk while Calico took a video of the whole thing. I drove back to Waaco, then put the bitch in the basement of one of the buildings. I circled her like a shark in murky waters, and she was terrified. Her name was Kim. I masked up and had Calico open the phone to call Remo. I held my gun to her head as he called Remo's FaceTime. He answered groggily.

"Fuck do you want, nigga?" he said, just waking up.

"I got your bitch, nigga. Give my money back or this hoe and your baby dead," I spat with venom.

He laughed hysterically. I was flustered with his response.

"I knew you were stupider than you look. Nigga, kill that bitch. I don't even know her, get somebody that matters," he said, then ended the call.

I couldn't believe my ears. This shit had me confused, but I figured this bitch-ass nigga was calling my bluff, so I called him again.

"Nigga, what? I'm tryin' to sleep. I got to spend yo' money early in the morning," he said.

I put the camera on her as I put the gun to her head and pulled the trigger. *Boom!* Her brains painted the wall, and he just chuckled and ended the call. I looked at Calico, confused; he simply shrugged.

"What about the baby?" Calico said.

I shook my head in defeat, I thought I was up on him . . .

(ZARO)

CUBANA LOUNGE...

Kamar and I sat in VIP talking. *Cubana* was a nice and elegant lounge; it was a quiet place where one could speak deliberately and make good, sound decisions. Kamar wanted to talk business.

"The streets is talking. I'm hearing you putting shit down hard right now," he said, blowing smoke circles from a thousand-dollar cigar.

I chuckled proudly at his gesture, then took a sip of the cognac.

"I'm close to needing to re-up on the powder," I said.

He smiled. "I'm sure you are, that's why I brought you here today. My guy Flacco got some serious weight, but he's out in California. How do you feel about working with him? He's got drivers and the whole shit."

"That's what I'm in it for. You just let me know what I gotta do."

"I'm throwing a party. It's going to be the premiere event of the year and everybody is gonna be there. I want you to be there so you can rub shoulders with the who's who in the hood. This party will put you where you need to be," he said.

Now I felt like I was really getting somewhere.

"I will be there, don't trip," I replied.

"On another note, I got this message about Flex last night. The boy you smoked a couple of weeks ago . . . well, he sent him," Unc said.

"That's funny because I got a list of addresses from Remo telling me where he laid his head and some other spots," I replied.

"I see he done pissed some people off," Unc said, affirming what I was already thinking. "What you gonna do with it is the question," he added.

"I'ma put it to work, ain't no question."

I planned on driving up to the address in Belvidere after I left the lounge. I had to go pick up my nigga—Zoo. If he wanted to become a real member of the team, today would be his chance to show what he was about with them pipes. He was loyal when it came to running the spot, but now I needed to see his trigger game. Kamar and I spent an hour longer at the lounge, the sun beginning to set around us.

I picked Zoo up around 8 p.m., as visiting hours were over at 8:30 p.m. at the hospital. I had to check on Cowboy before we left, and we made it just in time. Zoo and I split up as he ducked off to the cafeteria so I could be alone with Cowboy.

95

I eased to his bedside and took in the sight. Him lying there soundless made me feel like he was already dead. I had paid the bill to keep him alive on the vents for another month, but it was very expensive. I looked at him and wondered how the hell those guys knew what we'd had planned. It was gnawing at me. All I could remember was Bang telling me that Mick asked for me in the hallway that night. *How did Mick know?* I said to myself. Savon and Tif walked in abruptly, interrupting my thoughts.

"What you doing here?" she asked while she and Tif walked in.

I spun to face her. "I was just missing my brother," I said somberly.

"Me too, I make sure to check on him every day and night," she replied.

"What y'all got planned for the night?" I asked.

I cut my eye over at Tif and caught the bitch sizing me up. Why was she looking at me like that? She'd never given any of us the eye like that.

"We just finna go eat somewhere, you?" Savon said.

"You can join if you diggin' in them pockets," Tif interjected.

I don't know who this bitch thought I was, but the look she had in her eye was demanding. Savon stepped into the bathroom for a moment, leaving Tif and I alone. She inched closer to me and whispered in a hushed tone.

"I know y'all robbed that bank. You need to hit my hand with some. I've been playing the side for too long," she said vindictively.

I smirked. "So is this you trying to extort a mu'fuka or some? 'Cause I ain't robbed no bank, you tweaking shorty," I replied, looking around to see if anyone heard her.

"Nigga, please, I got you by five years. Savon don't know, but I'm sure if she finds out, this could possibly be why Cowboy is laying on that gurney. She would flip."

I couldn't believe this bitch was shaking me down. I dug into my pockets and gave her whatever I had. She stuffed the money in tiddy city.

"How much is it?" she asked.

"Bitch, I don't know. Prolly 3 bandz or some shit like that," I scoffed angrily.

The toilet flushed, and Savon stepped out.

"You want to go eat with us, Zaro?" Savon asked.

Tif had a dumb smirk on her face. "Yeah, you should come with us," she added with sarcasm.

"Nawl, I'm good, I all of a sudden feel sick. Maybe you and I can do some tomorrow night," I replied.

"Suit yourself, Imma hold you to it too. They got this new restaurant I wanna try."

I nodded, then looked at Cowboy, lying motionless on that bed.

We left the hospital around 9 p.m., with Zoo and I on the road to Belvidere, listening to Big30. I was in a zone; I wanted to kill somebody. My thoughts ran ballistic with the need to figure out who told Flex Neem my plan. Everything in the past few weeks ran through my head as I parsed the whole thing out. It was a lot to process. I read the address on my phone, matched it to the house, then saw the Range Rover. I turned the music down.

"That's their Range Rover," I said.

"You sure?" Zoo asked, looking at the house.

It was damn near a mansion, and not something you'd expect a nigga like Flex to live in. The lawn was well manicured, with a water fountain out front. There was another nice car in the driveway, a Tesla. As I squinted to get a better view, I noticed there was a sticker in the window, then I stopped.

"Can you see what that says?" I asked.

"Hold up," he said.

Zoo popped out the car, ran up to the Tesla, then hopped back in the Magnum winded. All he managed to say between breaths was, "It says *District Attorney*."

I drove back to Rockford with yet another problem on my plate. This shit was getting to be too much.

Next day...

"Bro, that bitch knows we robbed that bank," I said, pacing back and forth in the trap.

"I don't understand. You said she extorted you out of some money?" Telay asked.

"Gang, that bitch greasy," I replied.

Nylon and Bang just sat there un-fazed by what I had just told them. I called the meeting to get an understanding of our next move, and this shit was frustrating. That's when I had an epiphany that stopped me dead in my tracks.

"Aye, didn't you say a couple of weeks ago that you seen Tif in the mall with Flex?" I asked Bang.

"Yeah, me and Cowboy seen her walking through Bloomingdale's with the nigga, fa sho," he replied.

I shook my head. "That dirty bitch," I spat.

"What is it?" Telay asked, concerned.

"Tif put them niggas on us sooner than we'd expected. The night we chopped the money up in Cowboy's bedroom, I met her in the hallway, and she gave me this funny look. You know the walls over there are super thin, so she must've heard the conversation through the walls," I replied.

"Now that we know that, then what's next?" Telay asked.

Bang hopped out his chair angrily and ranted. "That bitch got to go, gang."

"Wait a minute, we don't know that for sure," Telay stated.

"DUH, DuDUH! It's Captain Save-a-Hoe to the rescue!" Nylon joked.

I knew what we had to do. It was all on me now. I'm the one who got us into this mess. I stood up to leave. We had to go check on Zoo anyway, and I had to contemplate my next move. In the meantime, though, I had to re-up. I called Shareef to let him know I would come through.

Hour's later...

Zoo and I pulled up to Shareef's spot and walked into the diner. I scanned the area, as I always did, while Channel brought me a menu that I never used. Zoo and I sat on the bar stools.

"One of these days you gon' have to try the food," Channel said.

I smiled and said, "How 'bout today?"

Shareef came from the back holding a to-go bag, which I knew had my dope inside.

"Aye, let me holla at you in the back, ocky," he said, and Channel walked off.

He gave Zoo a head nod like everything was okay, and we went to his office. Shareef sat on the edge of his desk and looked me square in the eye.

"Ock, this it right here. I only got enough for this re-up. We got a 3-month recession ahead of us to stay ahead of the game and keep my peoples on top. This the last of my shit right here. My other guy picked up already, so I wanna double your load to get you through the down period," he said.

I opened the bag and peeked inside. It was a whole kilo of raw. This was more than enough for me; I had moved up in the game.

I waved at Channel as we exited the diner, and I drove the product back to my aunt's. When I entered the house, Shiela met us at the door. The look she had was daggering...

"What's wrong?" I asked.

"These two policemen came by here today and left these cards. Said you need to speak with them ASAP."

I went toward the basement to stash the dope in the secret room and then read the two cards . . .

"Curly Abotts and Michael Coats," I muttered.

"What they want you for?" Zoo asked.

"It ain't shit, gang. If they really wanted me, I'd likely have a warrant or some shit."

I wonder if Tif opened her big-ass mouth, I thought to myself and hoped the bitch wasn't talking to twelve.

"You gon' go talk to them?" Zoo asked.

I broke a large chunk of the dope off, then stashed the rest before we left to go back to the trap house. I wasn't sure how to handle the situation with the cops. I dropped the pack off on Telay. *Vrm! Vrm! Vrm!* My phone buzzed. It was Savon. I answered and found out her car had broken down and she wanted me to give her a ride back to Waaco. I dropped Zoo with the dope at Rene's spot, then picked Savon up at the hospital. She slid into the Magnum with her face saturated with tears.

"What's going on? Is something wrong?" I asked, my face frowned up.

She nodded, her voice broken with fear. "The—they wa—want to pull the plug tomorrow," she said, fighting with sniffles.

"What? How's that? I don't get it. Kamar paid the bill for the life support."

"They saying it's unlikely he'll pull through."

"Damn, this shit is crazy. Will they give him a couple of days? Maybe if we all go show our support, you feel me?"

"That's good, it may work. My bro strong. I know he'll pull through."

My stomach growled. I hadn't had anything to eat all day.

"You want to get some late dinner?" I asked.

"Yeah, we can do that. I really need a drink," she admitted.

We ate at Olive Garden and reminisced on Cowboy and how funny he could be at times. I felt good sitting and just talking to her. Savon was something special. She was a diva like Beyoncé, her beauty mesmerizing, and when I looked into her hazel-colored eyes, my heart would skip a beat. She had creamy smooth skin and was built like an Instagram model. Savon had the 3 B's: Beauty, Body, and Brains. It was hard to believe her and Tif were cool. They were like apples to oranges. We left the restaurant, and I made my way to the liquor store and got us a bottle of Don Julio. It was surprising to me that she hadn't said anything about any money, which meant Tif hadn't said nothing yet. She gave me directions to Tif's new apartment, a small townhouse on the northside.

"You comin' in, ain't you?" she said.

"Nawl, I got some business to handle," I replied.

Savon slid out the front seat slowly. I wanted to hang out, but I had too much shit on my mind at the moment.

"I'll meet you at the hospital tomorrow," I said, then watched her walk to the door.

2 A.M. same night...

Tif parked her car in front of her townhouse, the street completely dark. I stepped out of the darkness as she went for her handbag in the back seat. She hadn't even noticed me standing behind her like Michael Myers.

"You need some help?" I asked.

She damn near jumped out her skin, then spun around.

"Oh shit! Boy, you scared the shit out of me," she said, startled, with her hand over her heart.

"My bad. What you afraid of?" I said, moving closer to her.

"Why you looking at me like that?"

She bent back over into the car looking for something as I pulled the F/N off my waist and pointed it at her head. I squeezed the trigger. *BOC! BOC! BOC!* And left her brains on the car seat. I threw my hood over my head and ran back to the Magnum.

"That's for you, Cowboy," I muttered as I crept off her block slow.

(FLEX)

Next night, SHAREEF'S DINER...

Calico and I sat in the Range Rover in the back alley of Shareef's diner as we waited on him to come out. He gave me this dumb spin move, saying he was busy and that there wasn't no work, but I knew better than that. He didn't have to lie to me; he'd said he sold his last brick to one of his people. Calico had that demon look in his eye as we listened to Tee Grizzley at a low thud. Calico turned towards me.

"Why would Shareef try to hold out on you? Y'all been doing business for a minute, and I don't see him getting down like that," Calico said.

"I do. This the dope game, nigga. This shit cut-throat; ain't no love or loyalty in it, you feel me," I replied.

I gripped my 10-milli and shifted in my seat. I could feel myself getting anxious. Calico was cold and calculated, and I knew having him with me would make shit go smooth as butter. The back door of the restaurant opened, and I perked up in my seat to get a better view.

"That's him. You ready, fam?" I asked.

He cocked his Glock 19 in response, so we stalked him like a snake does its prey. The car doors opened, and as we struck out towards him, I put the glizzy to his head.

"Don't move, nigga, or I'mma splatter your shit all over this muthafucking pavement," I said viciously.

Shareef stopped in his tracks and looked up.

"Ock, I know that's you. You don't have to do what you're doing . . . this me, dawg," he pleaded.

"Yeah, this nigga! This a glizzy now, where that work at?" I said with menacing eyes.

"Flex, think about what you're doing, my nigga. On Allah, you need to . . . you ain't got to do this, my nigga," Shareef said.

"Boy, you lied to me. You talking 'bout you ain't got shit. I been watching mu'fukas running through this bitch all day," I said with no remorse.

Shareef shook his head in defeat. "Flex, you ain't got to be like that. This a restaurant, and I run a business, ock. These are customers you're looking at coming through. Don't let that shit go to ya head, fam," he said, trying to be persuasive.

I stood with my gun drawn, looking at him and trying to figure out my next move when it hit me like a ton of bricks.

"Walk me to that stash or I'm gonna whack this bitch," I said, and right on cue, Calico showed back up with Channel, holding a 19 to her head. She cried a waterfall.

"Shut the fuck up, bitch, or I'mma put one of these hydro shocks in ya cap," I said with aggression.

"You ain't got to do that, ock."

This nigga was testing my patience, and I knew he was stalling me out. I had to end this lil' game before the feds pulled up, so I smacked him hard with the butt of my gun, and Calico and I walked him back inside the restaurant. He went to the kitchen and pulled out a large bag that looked like rice.

"You don't have to do this, ock."

I laughed. "Boy, look, this nigga talking this drought shit and you ain't got shit, huh!" I looked to Calico, and the stare he had told me the next move was on me. I turned back to Shareef, put the pipe to his temple, then said:

"You know I can't let you live, fam. You too tapped in." I pulled the trigger. *BOC! BOC! BOC!* The gun jerked in my hand.

Shareef collapsed to the ground, his body twitching as he fell to the bloodied tile. Calico rummaged through the bag of rice and pulled out ten packages wrapped in what appeared to be foil. They had come straight from overseas; the red writing on them was in Arabic. I smirked as I moved swiftly, putting the dope into a tote bag I'd scrounged up in the kitchen. Calico and I hit the back door like the Phantom of the Opera. We ran out with blocks of silver-wrapped Iran packages. I threw them in the trunk, and Calico and I drove off in the Range Rover, smooth as we'd come.

I drove to my house in Belvidere where we could stash the drugs. This was a huge lick for us; it was almost enough for me to forget about Remo, but he was still as good as dead in my book. I unlocked the doors to my home, and as we entered, I signaled for Calico to be quiet as I hung my key in the foyer. My home was sacred; I never brought my business home with me, but Calico and I were tighter than anybody. He was familiar with my place, so he made his way to the back where my game room was, as he'd been there before. I darted upstairs to let Kim know that I was home. Kim and I had been married for twelve long years, and we had three kids together. The twins—Vern and Veto—were 12, and our other son, Calvin, who was a special case as he was autistic, was 10. Kim wasn't a street chick. She worked as a prosecutor and was the reason I'd outlasted a lot of niggas in the streets. She also was the reason for the gang unit releasing Calico and I. Kim kept me up on police raids and snitches; she understood my street life and was fine with it—most of the time. I eased into the bedroom as she lay beneath the silk sheets. She moved slightly as I walked inside.

"Babe, is that you?" she asked.

"Yeah, babe, Calico and I are downstairs," I said, then kissed her softly.

She snickered, "You smell like the streets."

If she only knew that smell I had on me was death. Shareef's soul lingered on me, and when I took a whiff of myself, I chuckled. "If you need me, I'll be in the man cave," I said.

"What time is it?"

"4 a.m," I replied.

Calico had the bricks stacked up on the table when I walked into the room. I laughed, then rubbed my hands together greedily.

"We 'bout to make a lot of money on this play," I said.

"Yeah, but what we gon' do for a connect?" Calico replied.

He'd made a valuable point, though I wasn't thinking about any of that at the moment. I would cross that bridge when I got to it. Kamar was still open if he hadn't found out I'd put that hit on him, which Mikey and his dummy friend botched.

"This shit is pure dog food, fam. This ain't like what he was selling us, the potency is way stronger. We can re-brick this to at least 25 keys of pure," I said.

Calico chuckled.

"Too bad your lil' Puerto Rican bitch divorced you, now we ain't got a chemist to blend the shit."

I shook my head.

"I guess we got to improvise."

Kim had walked in while we had all the dope on the table. She looked at it, then asked what we wanted to eat for breakfast. She was already up, so there was no turning it down.

(ZARO)

Hospital vibe...

Savon's eyes were red and puffy from crying. She was going through a lot, with the doctors trying to kick Cowboy off the vents and her best friend having been murdered. Tif's funeral would be tomorrow, but no one could view the body anyway, due to the fact her head looked like an exploded pumpkin. Her and Tif had been friends for a long time, but if she'd known Tif had set her brother up, and on top of that, was trying to comfort her while extorting money from me.

she would feel the same as me. Maybe what I was doing didn't matter, seeing as I couldn't tell her I killed Tif, but it wouldn't be right if I didn't console her either.

"I don't know who would want to murder Tif," she said while sniffling.

I hugged her.

"She's in a better place now," I said in a comforting tone.

The doctor stepped in and interrupted us. He walked around the bed, checking the monitors and Cowboy's vitals.

"Doc, do you think he'll ever come out of this coma he's in?" I asked.

"Let's hope so. It's not a rare occurrence, but usually the patient would have come out by now. Your friend still has some motor skill function, though," the doctor explained.

"If that's the case, then why would you pull the plug on him?" I asked.

"It's been weeks that he's been on the vent. At this rate, he could be on here for months, maybe even years," he answered.

He tucked the clipboard under his arm, then exited the room. I felt like it was racism, but I couldn't prove it, of course. Savon didn't see what I asked; she had her head down, looking at her brother in deep thought.

"I got an idea. Let's both get something to eat," I said, looking at the clock. It was almost time for visiting hours to be over with.

"You want to go out and get a drink or something to get your mind off this bullshit that's going on?" I asked, trying to make Savon feel better. She was going through way too much right now, and I hated that for her. The least I could do was try to take her mind off it, even for a sec. Both her and I were spending a lot of time at the hospital with Cowboy, as Bang and the others were busy sieging the city from Waaco. I don't understand how the cookie crumbles, but I wasn't feeling any closer to getting Waaco. There were just too many of them niggas to eradicate.

Savon and I rode in my Magnum towards the sports bar. We sat and had drinks while watching Monday Night Football. I was mad; Justin Fields had thrown an interception. As we talked, I looked her in those eyes I yearned for. I didn't know exactly how to come out and say it, and I wasn't sure if it was even right, but Cowboy and I were friends, and she had always been like a big sister to me. I topped a stiff shot of Patron, then pulled out a wad of cash. She looked at the roll of all hundred-dollar bills.

"Looks like you been on the move," she said suspiciously.

"I'm just maintaining," I said nonchalantly to throw her off my trail.

She looked at me with twisted lips and a non-believing stare.

"Zaro, you got about 5 bands on hand. Is that money the reason my brother is in a coma? You not telling me something," she said, looking at me with pleading eyes.

I couldn't bear telling her the truth. I needed to divert our conversation; the waitress walked up in perfect timing as she set our drinks in front of us. I seized the moment and asked the first thing that came to mind.

"Do you guys have any chicken wings?"

Savon smiled and shook her head. She'd known I was trying to avoid the topic.

"We have a wide variety of wings, ten different flavors," she replied, then she went into a long, drawn-out spiel about the wings I didn't care to hear.

Savon giggled. "I'll have a fish platter," she said, interrupting the waitress's chicken speech.

I laughed at her candor. I cut my eye to the left and noticed one of Waaco's crew members. I hoped he didn't see me as I tried turning my head sideways.

"Is something wrong?" Savon asked, noticing my mood change.

"You want to get out of here?" I said and started looking around for another exit.

"Are you okay? Why you acting like that?"

I looked over in Rick's direction. Savon caught my glare. She leaned in closer to me and, in a hushed tone, said:

"Zaro, tell me what's going on. You're scaring me with all this secretive shit."

Rick had his eyes glued to me when he suddenly got on his phone. I was sure he was calling for backup, and they were probably waiting on me outside by now. I had to tell Savon what was happening. I couldn't let anything happen to her.

I scoffed heavily.

"I'm beefing with Waaco. After they shot Cowboy, we've been getting back at them."

She looked at me in disbelief. It was a portion of the truth, though, and this would have to suffice for now. Her eyes were angered. She'd already known Mick had pulled the trigger on Cowboy, with no clue as to why.

She finally spoke.

"How are we 'bout to get out of here?" she asked.

"I'mma need you to get my gun out the car for me. It's underneath the driver seat," I said.

She nodded. I was sure there were more goons outside. I made the call to Zoo and Bang to help me out; it was my only chance to get out of here alive. I dialed Bang's number while Savon trotted off to the car. She was back in minutes, and I met her in the bathroom where she passed me my Glock 10 with a switch. I popped in the 30-round clip and jacked the slide. I was ready for whatever came my way now. I put the pipe on my waistline, then we both eased out of the restroom.

The bar was packed with patrons. I knew Rick wouldn't try to make a move inside the bar. I scanned the area to get a visual on Rick's whereabouts, but he wasn't in the same place I'd last seen him. I noticed him in the corner, looking around for me.

"What do we do now?" Savon asked, holding on tight to my hand. I could feel her energy transferring into me.

"Bang Neem should be here soon. I don't think he'll try anything on you, so it should be okay for you to leave. I can handle these goofy-ass niggas on my own."

"I'm with you. We gone make it out of here together," she exclaimed.

Moments later, Zoo sent me a text. Rick most likely didn't have a gun—at least I thought against it, based on the fact they were checking for weapons at the door. My phone pinged again. I read it: Zoo had arrived, and they were parked out front. I rose from my seat as Rick moved toward me with a bottle in hand. I stood up defensively, then pulled out the Glock 10. He stopped in his tracks, then nodded and smirked.

"This ain't what you want, my boy," I said.

"We gone catch yo goofy ass, boy," he said, then backed off.

I backed out the club, keeping my eye on Rick until I stepped outside. As I searched around for Zoo, I noticed the Range Rover in the cut. The headlights came on. I instructed Savon to run, and we broke out toward the Magnum.

FIT! FIT! FIT! FIT! FIT! FIT! The sound of gunfire erupted all around us, sounding like a night in Gaza.

I hit the switch on my G10. *FA! FA! FA! FA! FA! FOW! Dadadadadadaow!*

THE GLIZY DANCED. I emptied all 30 rounds in one second, then glanced at Zoo. He had an Army-issued M16 with a box clip. Waaco didn't stand a chance. Zoo dropped Rick as he ran out the bar. I climbed into the car. Savon screamed as bullets struck the car's exterior. I laughed as nothing penetrated.

I floored the Magnum. The Hellafant roared as it came full of life. My tires burned the pavement, making a loud screeching noise that sounded like a wild banshee screaming down the block. I drove from the scene in a rush, turning East State Street into a NASCAR racetrack.

Savon gripped the door panel.

"What the fuck? I can hear the bullets hit the car; we should be dead," she said, frantic but calming.

"The car is bullet-proof, windows and all," I replied.

"What have y'all gotten into?"

I felt bad for keeping this new lifestyle from her, but I promised myself I would tell her tomorrow, as they were scheduled to pull the plug on Cowboy at 6 p.m. I had to come clean after that. Hopefully, she wouldn't blame me for Cowboy's death, even though it was my fault.

Zoo texted my phone, and I replied with the thumbs-up emoji.

"Let me take you to get some food," I asked.

"I don't know . . . is it safe?" she chuckled. "It's been an eventful night. Where we headed?"

"Shareef's Diner—they sell the best authentic Arabic food you'll ever taste," I replied.

"You sure they're open right now? It's really late."

I checked the time; it was 3 a.m. as I pulled up and circled around the block. I noticed Flex's Range Rover in the alley. He and Calico came out, threw something in the trunk, and rode off fast. I had in mind to follow him—this was my time to get a good location on where he might be resting his head.

Savon was oblivious to what was going on. I followed them down the highway until we reached Belvidere, when she asked, "Where are we going? It's getting late."

"I want to stop off at a Denny's," I answered.

She laid her head back to get some rest, as I followed Flex all the way to a large Victorian-style house. This had to be the same address I'd gotten from Remo.

"Gotch yo' ass," I muttered, then drove back to Rockford. We stopped at Denny's and got a to-go bag. Savon spent the night with me at my spot.

The house was dark and empty.

"Where's your aunt?" she asked.

"Gone for the night. We alone," I chuckled.

I led her to the guest room, still mesmerized by her hazel-brown eyes. I lusted for her body—her Instagram-model body with creamy-colored yellow skin that drove me crazy. We stood inches apart, her breasts perked up on my chest. I could feel the energy she emitted.

"I want you to sleep with me," she said softly. Her voice gave me an instant erection inside my Ethika drawers. She pressed herself to me, then planted a soft, wet kiss on my lips. Her touch was electrifying. I scooped her up by her bottom as we kissed passionately. I couldn't believe this was happening.

I sat her on the bed as we broke apart, then she lustfully slipped her Dolce & Gabbana shirt over her head, her breasts perked in her bra as she freed them. I looked at the prize in front of me: her nipples, shaped like almonds, rested perfectly on her melons. I began by snaking my tongue over them as she moaned lightly. When I tugged at her pants, she wiggled herself out of her jeans. I stood in front of her, looking down at her clean-shaven pussy; she had a camel toe between her legs. She licked her finger, then slid it into the crevasses of her pussy—it slid in easily. I put my face between her box, then went to work. I had way too much built-up cum for her, so there was no need for Henny or Blue-Chew; her juices flowed like the Mississippi River.

"Oh yes, lick this pussy, daddy, I need you!" she groaned and begged.

My dick head fought with my underwear to escape its cage. I stood up, slid my underwear off, and my rod popped up and out. Savon slid back on the bed in a comfortable position and gazed at my pole with a sultry stare. I moved over to the side of the bed. As she came within 10 inches of me, eye to eye, she devoured me like an OnlyFans model. I tilted my head back in pleasure.

"Damn, baby," I said.

The slurping sounds alone made my toes curl. When she looked up at me and asked, "Where you gone nut, daddy?"

"Not now, baby. I got to see what that pussy's like," I answered with a grunt.

She continued to suck on me, the whites of her eyes seductive as she gazed up at me. With every stare, my pipe came alive in her mouth. I just had to feel her pussy. I could feel the tingle inside my scrotum, so I backed up, ejecting myself from the warmth of her succulent lips.

"Uhmm!" she moaned with a seductive look in her eye. I believe it was her looks that had me feeling the way I did. She laid on her back, inviting me in to explore her love button further. I let my dick head massage her clit, then rubbed it across her vulva. With every motion, she yearned to feel me inside her. I finally gave her what her body desired; her wet pussy sucked me in like a vortex.

"Oh yes, give me the dick!"

I teased her with slow strokes, using my head to paint her walls with my precum.

"Arhhh!" I grunted pleasurably.

I was in a land of ecstasy. I stroked her with slow, teasing strokes first, then went fast. I howled and grunted as I pushed even deeper.

"OWEEEEEEEE!" she howled. I flipped her over and mounted her from the back, her ass fat and jiggly like jelly. I squeezed her cheeks, then pounded her back in.

"Oh yes, yes, yes, right there," she said, begging me to keep hitting the same spot, enough to wake the neighbors.

I let lose my load, my body trembling as I drained myself of every drop of cum I had in me. We fell asleep within seconds. She lay next to me with a light snore.

Vrm! Vrm! Vrm! I woke up to my phone buzzing. I checked the ID, it read Kamar. I set the phone back down, figuring I could get up with him later. For now, I would enjoy the moment. She rolled over and put her arm around me as I kissed her softly. I set the phone back on the nightstand and closed my eyes.

Vrm! Vrm! Vrm! It buzzed again.

I huffed, frustrated, then answered.

"Unc, it's early as fuck and I had a long night," I answered.

"I need you at my office ASAP," he said in a serious tone.

I sat up straight in the bed with a bewildered look.

"What's going on?" I asked.

"Just get here now, don't make me wait," he said, then ended the call abruptly. I looked at the blank screen offensively.

Savon peered at me.

"What's going on? Is everything alright?" she asked.

"I don't know. I got some' to handle."

"What if Sheila comes back?" she asked.

I chuckled. "Baby, please, you good. My aunt loves you," I said, then kissed her as I got up.

I slid on my clothes, grabbed my gun, and hit the door. I called Zoo, letting him know I was about to scoop him up and that I needed him to ride with me. I trusted unc, but trust would get you killed.

Zoo had twin Glock 23's in his lap as we rode down West State Street.

"What we about to get into, my baby?" he asked.

"I don't know, Unc called me like something was up. I just don't want to run up on no dumb shit, ya feel me? So be ready to squeeze if need be."

Zoo nodded. Since he'd been sliding with us, he'd put in his fair share of work. All my niggas were playing their parts: Bang and Nylon moving the d-line at Rene's, while Telay and Zoo moved the coke, doing numbers at an Eastside spot I rented.

I pulled up to the car lot. I gaped around at all the black Trackhawks parked at the door. A Rolls truck sat at the helm of the motorcade, all bearing diplomatic plates.

"Fuck is going on here?" I muttered as I drove around the lot.

"What's good, gang? You looking like something wrong," Zoo said, turning his head in search of nothing in particular.

"I don't know," I replied with caution.

Zoo and I both exited the Magnum in unison as I scanned the area on our way to the door. The truck's drivers were all seated, their stares blank and menacing. They wore bow ties, big beards, and bald heads; the atmosphere was off. I could feel tension in the air as I walked to the door. Two large men stood posted in our path.

"What's your business here?" the brute of a man asked with a foreign accent.

I guessed he was of Arabic descent. They were all positioned around the lobby of Kamar's spot, and I was appalled by his aggressiveness towards me. I was invited here. I felt disrespected by their rudeness, but the bulges inside their jackets let me know they were heavily armed. Zoo and I had our weapons tucked, but thankfully Kamar came walking from the back and stopped in the hallway.

"Let him back," he said.

Zoo faced me with discernment in his gaze. I was thrown off by it myself.

"Come on, we don't have all day," Kamar said. I had never seen Unc look the way he did. Kamar was usually calm and in control; this was different.

I looked at Zoo, then said.

"It's good, fam, I'll be aight."

I followed Kamar through the hallway as we pushed past the bow-tie men, who were like gargoyle statues. I entered cautiously into the office. A tall, lanky man was seated in the chair, his legs crossed. He was dressed down in Arabian desert attire with a long, graying beard. His turban gave him the Bin Laden appearance.

"Have a seat," Kamar said, sitting on the edge of the desk. He looked at me with a piercing gaze.

"What's going on, Unc? You got me nervous right now," I said, cutting my eye to the guy who sat silently.

"Nervous why? Do you have something to hide?" He looked at me figuratively.

"What are you getting at? I'm at a loss, Unc. All these riddles got me feeling real uneasy."

"Last night, Shareef was murdered," he said sharply.

Kamar and the mystery guy both stared at me for a reaction. I shook my head, disappointed that something like this had occurred, although I wasn't sure why he'd called me—I wasn't there.

"I wasn't there, Unc. I can't help you. Shareef was my nigga, and I would never cross him like that, or you, for that fact."

He cut me off.

"I ain't say all that, but we got to get to the bottom of this shit. Shareef was a major nigga out here."

The mystery man had a sinister glare about him, his aura seemed diabolical as he sized me up, then spoke.

"My name is Saleem. Shareef was my nephew. We are here on business. After viewing your name in his book of clients, he'd made record you picked up 1 kilo that day. Am I correct?" he spoke in an Arabic dialect, his English broken but salvageable.

Why the fuck would they have me in a ready-made conspiracy for the cops to find? I didn't know how to answer the question, but I knew this wasn't the time to be playing around with the "I don't know what you're talking about" routine.

"He and I did business, and that was that. I had no reason to kill him," I said before it dawned on me about last night with Flex.

"We have footage of your car riding past. You followed another truck away from the scene," he asked.

I was feeling fucked up at first, that me and Flex had the same connect, but this was my time to cut him out the loop.

"I saw Flex and Calico exit the restaurant in a hurry last night. The place was closed. I followed him to get a better advantage over him, as he and I are opps," I proclaimed.

"Opps? What does this mean?" he asked curiously.

"I want to kill him."

He looked me in the eye for some sort of sign, but I was genuine.

"I trust Zaro. He is a good friend and a valued client to this organization," Kamar spoke on my behalf.

"Take me to where you followed him. I went through my phone and brought up the location.

"Thank you for your help," the man said then rose from his seat and shook hands with Kamar. He exited the office on a hunt for Flex. I chuckled knowing Waaco was 'bout to heat up, as these men looked like straight terrorists.

(O'RILEY)

POOL HALL...

It had been a week since the meeting at the motel. Marty was worried that Bruiser's guy had made him for an informant, but I assured Marty all was well. I drove us to the pool hall to meet Bruiser. The first load of meth was ready as I parked in the back alley. Motorcycles littered the area, clogging the parking lot; it got Marty looking nervous.

"You got to ease up or else they'll make us for cops. Stop what you're doing, now," I commanded.

"What if this shit goes sour for some reason?" he said.

I pulled my gun and laid it in my lap. "We ain't got shit to worry about, now beat your feet. And for the last time, you're paranoid! The guy ain't said shit, so why would they have us here to pick up the first load? Now let's go."

We slid out the Benz and walked to the door where Bruiser met us in the back with a duffle bag. He passed it to me through the door without letting me in. I stood in the alley, appalled as we walked back to the car.

"I told you something is up," Marty said.

"Will you shut the hell up, let me think about this shit," I said, and laid the bag in the trunk...

I checked the contents, and it was full of meth like I'd hoped. Those bikers were tweaking off their own product, they were just tweaking, I told myself as I drove out the alley and headed back to the pub.

I hid the work in the back of the bar. Vrm, Vrm, Vrm, my phone buzzed. The screen read O'Mally. I looked around to make sure I was out of Marty's earshot.

"Hello," I answered.

"Did you take care of him yet?" he asked.

"It will get done," I said, and O'Mally ended the call abruptly.

I knew what I had to do. It was funny how a man could feel death looming in his presence. Marty knew something was amiss, but I had to get rid of him as it was either him or me. Marty was right, Steve was onto him, and I had to take care of Marty; it was the only way I could prove my loyalty to the mob. I stepped back into the bar, and Marty was gone. He texted my phone. The message read [be back, gotta make a quick]

I nodded. I'd take care of Marty when he got back.

(MARTY)

ABOTTS' meeting spot...

I set up a secret meet with Curly, away from O'Riley. I was starting to not trust O'Riley anymore. He was too overly easy about what was going on. We met in our usual spot, and Curly was already backed into the parking stall. I backed in, window to window with his Impala. The park was vacant. I looked over to Curly with desperate, pleading eyes.

"What you got for me?" Curly asked.

"The bikers are moving meth into the city, among other things. I need protection. O'Riley isn't with us anymore."

"We gonna need you to testify on O'Riley. We got him for the murder of Roger, so what else do you got that will stick?"

"There's about 20 pounds of meth at the club now," I admitted.

O'Riley and I were like brothers, but one thing I knew was that he was capable of killing someone close to him. He'd been trying to talk my guard down, but I was on high alert.

"Okay, is there anything else? What about that Zaro kid?" Curly asked.

"O'Riley gave him an arsenal of guns, so he's the reason behind the spike in crime. O'Riley messed up by giving him those weapons. Zaro has been at odds with Flex," I said, though Curly seemed particularly interested in Zaro.

Abotts took notes as I snitched out everyone. I'm sure the IRA would have me killed for what I was doing, but self-preservation was the name of the game, and I wasn't going out like a shmuck. I'd rather hide out in witness protection for the rest of my life at this point. I was ready to rat on the IRA and anyone else in my path.

"O'Riley has the drugs at the pub right now?" Abotts asked, anxious to make the bust.

"It's there, along with a supply of guns from the Chicago freight."

"Good boy, Marty."

I looked up as a van screeched its tires in front of my car, blocking my exit. The door slid open, and my heart skipped a beat. Three masked men hopped out, wheeling a high-powered .50 Cal.

Lalalalalalalaow! The shell casings sounded like pop cans hitting the pavement; bullets ripped through my Benz like it was made of paper. The windshield shattered, glass rained all around me . . .

Tish, Tish, Tish! I tried to shield my head from the imminent threat of danger.

I heard Curly frantically yelling into his radio.

"Shots fired! Shots fired! Officer needs assistance!" he repeated over and over, each time more aggressive than the last.

Curly's voice became fainter as I could feel a warm ooze soaking my shirt. I looked down at my chest and panicked. My breathing became erratic as I put my hand over my chest to feel the hole in my heart. Applying pressure had become futile. I stared, fading out. The paramedics' voice talking fast to save me had become faint. The last thing I heard was:

"I need crash cart . . . he's going into cardiac. Hit him with the epi."

Suddenly, the beams of light decreed upon my soul; the reaper had come for me . . .

(O'RILEY)

Hours later...

I packed all my shit in a rush. The IRA was coming for me after hearing the news of Marty's untimely death. It could only mean one thing: O'Mally didn't trust me to take care of the hit, or it was a double cross to get me; either way, I wasn't taking any chances. I had to get out of Dodge before I was next. I was flabbergasted by the fact that Marty was having a secret meeting with Curly, though it was no concern at the moment. I hurriedly moved about the bar, gathering items. We were closed, and no one knew I was getting as far away from Rockford as possible.

I grabbed the duffle bag of meth that I'd gotten from Bruiser; this would be my new beginning while I was on the run. It was enough dope for anyone. I threw the bag over my shoulder, then headed for the door when I heard a loud crash and patters of feet upstairs.

"Oh shit, they're here," I muttered and turned for the secret exit. Suddenly, I heard that door being pried open. The doors were crashing in all around me as I heard those fatal words: FBI. The SWAT team had closed in on me as I stood in the middle of the card room and awaited my fate. I was thrown to the ground and cuffed. I squirmed on the ground like a fish out of water. I smirked, knowing I had the get-out-of-jail free card.

"Call Detective Curly Abotts, I'm his informant," I said, trying to weasel my way out of the corner I was backed into.

The masked agent had me pinned down. "It's over," O'Mally said, sliding the mask off his head.

I looked over to see Coats' ugly mug.

"Pick him up," he said with an empathetic tone. "It's over with. The Fighting Irish is out of fight," Abotts said, delivering me a lethal dose of reality.

I shook my head in defeat. It was all too much for me to swallow. There was no way I could go to jail—I would be killed within hours.

"You can't take me. I'll be killed the minute you put me on the inside. Besides, I got a lot to offer. Let me make it up, and I'll give you whoever you want. I got the robbery suspects," I pleaded.

Abotts looked cynical as he laughed, and it sounded sinister. I'd never seen him this upset.

"You almost got me and Coats killed in that little hit you orchestrated on Marty today."

"Wait, I had nothing to do with that. Give me a chance to explain," I replied.

Coats was busy going through my tote bag, as he pulled out the pounds of meth. The other officers found the armory of weapons, which was enough to get me a life sentence in itself. My world was crashing down in front of me.

"Looks like you got a lot of talking to do," Coats interjected.

I was cuffed and put in the back of a squad car...

(ABOTTS)

POLICE STATION...

Coats walked into our small cubicle in the station. We had all the evidence on O'Mally laid out on the table; it was a huge seizure for us. Coats laid a packet of meth in front of me, and I picked it up then examined it.

"What's the purity level? Enough for life, I hope?"

Coats chuckled. "It's enough salt to take your life," he said.

"What!"

"It's all salt. The test came back and it's rock salt," he said, then plopped down into his chair.

"We at least got him on the guns and the murder of Roger."

"How do you want to approach the situation? We can't let him get away with the murder," Coats replied.

"Let's start with what he could give us on Zaro. We got to secure a warrant on him. His name has come up in too much shit in the past few weeks."

"Are we offering O'Mally some sort of immunity deal?" Coats asked.

"Fuck no! We're gonna stick it to him hard, but let him give us what we want first."

"You're cold for that," Coats stated, then smirked.

"We're gonna let his ass sit in the county for a few days before we decide to talk to him. That way he'll have a lot of thought-out information to give us, versus scattered-out bullshit."

I sat back. My game plan was set. All these motherfuckers were about to go down at O'Mally's expense.

(O'MALLY)

WINNEBAGO COUNTY JAIL...

I paced a hole in the floor. I ran to the bars every time a guard came, hoping Abotts had sent for me. After no luck, I took a seat back on the bench.

"I got to get out of here," I muttered. The walls were starting to close in on me as I picked up the phone to call Abotts. I was informed he was out of office, and I dropped my head. I was literally a rat backed into a wall, and I regretted doing business with the police in the first place; it was the worst decision of my life.

I heard keys jingling towards the holding cell, and I jumped up anxiously as the guard opened the gate and let a biker-looking guy in. He was heavyset with a long, thick beard, and I cracked my knuckles to prepare for an altercation if any came. The man mugged me as he walked in.

"C/O, I want my free call," I asked, hoping to get out the cell so I could let the guard know I had info. I need them to put me in PC, as it was dangerous for me to be sitting here.

"You got to wait your turn like everyone else," he said firmly.

I started to pace the floor as he locked the gate back. The new arrival laid back on the bench, reeking of booze. In minutes, he snored like a grizzly bear. He looked harmless, but there was no way to tell, and my paranoia had begun to sink in.

We'd sit in the holding cell for hours before the guards processed us into general population. We were given a lice shower, then led to the pods. By that time, the jail was locked down for the night. I hoped to speak with Abotts or Coats tomorrow.

"You two ladies are both going to room 217," the C/O said, looking down at an index card.

I was somewhat relieved—at least they weren't throwing me on some unsuspecting schmuck in the middle of the night. I looked over at the guy to see if he opposed to our new living arrangements. We'd been in the holding cell all day together, and I'd never even asked his name.

"What's your name?" I asked as we both dropped our bedrolls on the lower bunk.

"Ralph," he responded with a long, tired yawn.

"I'm Riley," I replied, hoping he hadn't heard anything about me.

We both eyed the lower bunk, waiting on the other to break the ice over who would have the bottom rack for the night.

"You want to rock-paper-scissors for the bed?" I asked with a smile.

"Nah, champ. Go for it. Hopefully, I'm just passing through," he said in a raspy tone, then climbed on the top bed without even laying sheets on it.

"Thanks, lad. I got a bad back, and I'm scared of heights," I said jokingly.

Ralph laughed, laid back, then balled himself beneath the wool blankets. He and I conversed a bit before we fell asleep. I found out he was in for a DUI and worked at a lumber yard. Ralph was an upstanding citizen, and I could rest easier knowing he wasn't part of any crime syndicate, biker club, or any type of illicit gang.

The day had literally drained me. I dreamed about Marty. His death was playing on my conscience, even though his murder wasn't by my hand. I empathized about it. Marty had ducked my bullet, only to get hit by the bikers, most likely. There was no real way for me to know, but O'Mally had left me with no other choice. Steve had to have let O'Mally know Marty was an informant.

Bruiser wanted my bar, and I felt O'Mally played the whole situation to his advantage and sold us to the bikers for the meth. I lay back and thought long about how Marty and I got back-doored by O'Mally. The morning came rather quickly. As I rose out of bed and got my breakfast, I looked at the shit they slopped on my tray in disgust—it was a horrible sight. I shook my head and offered it to Ralph. He must've been hungry, because he scarfed it down in a hurry.

I looked around for the phones; I had to get a hold of Abotts. I couldn't stay in here too long.

(FLEX)

Days later...
Calico and I had to shake all the drugs ourselves, as Remo was out of the picture. I had enough dope to keep the projects heavy for a while, but we had no connect. I'd be up a cool million in the game after I was done with the keys I had from Shareef, though. I looked to Calico, then said, "You ever wonder how much money is enough money?"

He chuckled. "What you tryin' to say, fam?"

"I'm sayin' we got ten keys off Shareef; that's over a mill in the building, we got choppers and switches all round. This might be a means to an end. You ever think of that?" I said, then tossed a finished bundle in the pile.

"I'm with you 'til the casket, gang, but the streets is all I know. You think niggas gonna respect us if we ain't in the field?"

"We ain't gotta leave the field. Let's open a club or something," I said, then took a deep pull from the wood.

"Or how about a dispensary? We can stay in the game and maybe find a plug. This fentanyl is about to take the world over, gang, and we need to rub shoulders with some respectful niggas. Ya boy Kamar did it. He got the car lot doin' good, and that nigga still dabb in the streets with all the major connects. He got politicians and all. That's where you need to be, big dawg," Calico said as I listened. He planted some good seeds in my brain. I passed the backwood to him...

"I think this is my last run, my baby. We need to really think about what we gon' do after this," I said.

Calico shook his head. "Well, you can turn Waaco over to me. Thunder 'bout to get outta prison, and he gon' need somethin' to fall back on."

Vrm, vrm, vrm, my phone buzzed. I answered. It was my wife; she told me Calvin was sick, and I had to rush home. I ended the call and stood to leave.

124

"You think you can handle this over here? I gotta make a run home," I said and snatched up my keys.

"Take care of your business, fam. I'm good over here."

I drove out the projects and noticed there was a lot of Muslims out walkin'. They were dressed in suits and bow ties, sellin' oils and incense. I looked at them, twisted my lip, and chuckled.

"Niggas is so disrespectful. These muthafuckas is relentless," I said, shaking my head as I punched the gas outta Waaco. I drove home doin' the dash, whipped into the driveway, and ran to the door.

"Calvin!" I shouted out for my son. I wasn't sure if Kim had taken him to the hospital yet. My guess was that he was havin' a mental breakdown. Calvin was my autistic son, and he needed me to get him outta his episodes.

"We in here!" Kim shouted from the dining room. I made my way past the living room. The house was unusually quiet. The twins were always runnin' through the house with their basketball. I got to the dining room and my heart dropped. I almost fell to my knees.

"How nice of you to join us," Saleen hissed.

I spun around, then two large men with Glocks blocked my path. One pressed the barrel of his gun to my head. "Move and you're dead," he said in a menacing tone.

I gazed into the men's eyes, and it was like they weren't human. I'd dealt with the most diabolical men in the game, but these men were a different type. As I looked at them, "terrorists" came to mind. I felt like the guy in front of me could've had something to do with 9/11. My skin crawled at his sight. He pointed a silenced Glock 29 in my direction . . .

(CALICO)

WAACO...

125

I finished baggin' up the last of the bundles when one of the lookouts, named Scooter, stepped into the small apartment.

"What are we gon' do about this infestation of Muslims? We got them out here pushin' their oils and shit. These niggas is in our way, gang. They all over the place harassin' the J's and shit," he said. I went to the window to check out what he was talkin' about.

I gawked at them walkin' through the projects, stoppin' all the customers. Then they started shoutin' in unison, "Allahu Akbar! Allahu Akbar!" I sat back down.

"What you wanna do?" Scooter asked, awaitin' my order . . . *Knock! Knock! Knock!*

"Start by gettin' the door, nigga," I replied.

Moments later, I heard somethin' hit the floor...

"Fuck is goin' on?" I asked, gettin' to my feet. I went to see what the loud thud was, and Scooter lay on the floor in a pool of blood. The gunmen turned towards me, lookin' to be Muslim, and trained his gun in my direction. *Pew! Pew! Pew!* Bullets pierced the walls as I backed out the hallway and ran to the living room to snatch the Draco from the couch.

Dadadadadadadad! The Draco danced as I painted the apartment with 7.2's. The man ducked behind a wall.

Pew! Pew! Pew! . . . He and I exchanged shots in the small apartment. The Muslim gunman was a trained shot, though. His bullets exited the barrel with precision, as I emptied my clips wildly. Eventually, I was struck by a bullet. I was boxed in. I threw the chop and ran for the window. I hopped out the second-story window without thinkin' and was lucky to land on an old mattress. I limped off, lookin' for some place to hide. I looked up to see the shooter pointin' in my direction . . . "There . . . there . . . right there!" he shouted.

The Muslims had opened fire on all the Waaco members. We were caught by total surprise. The gunmen were on the hunt. I had to find some place to hide. I limped over to the dumpster and dove inside. The smell of nasty diapers and rotten food made my stomach churn. My stomach muscles jerked as I caught my vomit. I listened to the gunfire rip through the air around me. Waaco had turned into a night in Ukraine. I lay in a heap of trash tryin' to figure a way outta the situation. We were under attack by what appeared to be terrorists, and I had to wait it out like a coward. "Where the fuck is Flex?" I thought as sharp pain struck in my leg. It had begun to throb as I lay crammed inside. I needed to stretch. After ten minutes of gunfire, the shots subsided and I opened the lid. As I scanned the area, I saw bodies everywhere. Waaco was dismembered. Suddenly, I heard one of the men say somethin' . . . "Find him," he demanded in a foreign accent.

I ducked back into my hiding spot, then tried to call Flex. The rings went unanswered. "Fuck!" I uttered.

I thought to call my cousin Crystal, as she would pick me up. Blood was oozing from my side and I was in desperate need of a doctor, so I dialed her number. She agreed to pick me up. Twenty minutes later, my phone buzzed, and I hurriedly answered it without lookin'.

"Hello . . . Hello . . . Hello?" I said in a whisper.

"I'm out here, where you at?" she asked. "Oh my god, what is all the police doin' out here? What happened?" Her voice trailed with astonishment.

"I'm in the dumpster in the back building."

She laughed hysterically. "Are you serious?" she said, then regained herself.

"Yes, now just get here please. Back up to the end dumpster under the trees; it's at the foot of the hill. Pop your trunk, and I'm gonna climb inside. Then drive straight to the hospital," I said between painful groans.

Crystal complied with my directive. She drove slow with me in the trunk. She kept her phone on, talkin' to me.

"There is a lot of police out here. Hold up. They got a roadblock," she said. I could hear her puttin' her phone down.

127

I listened to the background and heard one of the cops say he was Homeland Security. Twenty minutes passed and we pulled into the emergency room at Rockford Memorial. She popped the trunk, and I limped out. She threw my arm over her shoulder and we walked to the entrance.

"Oh my god, you stink," she said, pluggin' her nose.

When I got to the sliding doors, my heart skipped a beat.

"Turn around, take me back to the car, hurry up before they see me!" I pleaded.

"What is goin' on with you?" she asked.

I was terrified. There was one of the Muslim men standin' inside the hospital. "Were they here for me?" I thought; either way, I was gettin' outta there. I slid into the front seat and laid the seat all the way back.

"Hurry up and get away from here," I warned.

"Who are those men? And why are you so afraid of them?" she demanded.

"They're the ones who shot up everything in Waaco," I replied with a crackle in my voice.

Her eyes bucked, and I nodded in unison. "You got to take me to your house. I ain't got nowhere to go, fam."

She scoffed. "I don't know, cuz. I don't want you to bring no shit my way. I can't afford to lose my job at the hospital," she shot back.

"You won't even know I'm there, I promise. I need you to dress my wound with that shit at your job. There's no way I can go to the hospital right now; they onto me, fam."

"Alright, but don't be smoking in my shit."

(ZARO)

Later that night...

Vrm! Vrm! Vrm! Savon's phone buzzed. I turned the music down so she could hear. She ended the call with, "I'm on my way." The call sounded important.

She looked over at me. "It was the hospital. They want us to get there as quick as possible."

My heart jolted. The first thing I thought was they'd pulled the plug on him early. I shook my head, feeling defeated.

"What did they say?" I asked.

"His condition has changed."

"Is it bad or worse?"

"I'm not sure," she answered.

I was already driving in that direction, so I pulled up minutes later. We hopped out and raced inside. We ran through the lobby, past the receptionist desk, and up the elevator. The ICU was on the fourth floor. We sprinted past the nurse's station to Cowboy's room, and I was shocked to see that no one was there. Savon gasped tearfully and put her hands over her mouth.

"No . . . no . . . nooo . . . please don't let us be too late," she cried.

I went to the nurse's station. "My brother was just in room 26, where did he go?" I asked.

The woman swiped the keys on her laptop, then peered at the screen. "Uhm . . . I'm not sure . . ." she said hesitantly.

"They literally just called me," Savon barked.

"Ma'am, please calm down. I will find your brother," the woman said.

"You looking for the guy that was in the coma?" another nurse who walked up asked.

"Yes," Savon shot back.

"They took him to recovery down on the 3rd floor. I'll show you," she said, then led the way.

Savon and I looked at each other excitedly. "Are you sure?" Savon asked.

"I'm positive," the woman replied.

We looked at the short, thick lady like a godsend angel from above. It could only mean that Cowboy was out of his coma. I was eager to get to the 3rd floor. We rode the elevator down in anticipation and were led to his new room. Cowboy lay on the gurney, eating Jell-O.

"Where y'all been?" he asked, smiling like nothing had happened.

Savon covered her mouth. "Oh my god, you're alive, I . . . I . . . I . . . thought you were dead," she said, struggling to muster words.

I looked at him with a grin, and we shook hands. I was sure he had a lot of questions for me, but I was glad he was back with us. It would have been hard for me to handle his death. Dr. Martin stepped in to update us on his health.

"How is he, doc?" I asked.

He looked down at his clipboard. "He should make a full recovery with some minor complications, but overall, with a little therapy, he'll be fine. There's a bullet lodged in his hip, but we have the perfect therapist that will help with his recovery. Her name is Crystal," he said, looking at Cowboy over his glasses.

"Hopefully, Crystal looks better than you, doc," Cowboy joked.

He chuckled and continued to read over his notes, giving us Cowboy's prognosis. I listened closely. *Vrm! Vrm! Vrm!* My phone buzzed, interrupting the doc as he spoke. I looked at the screen; it read Kamar.

"Can you excuse me for a moment? I have to take this call," I said and stepped into the hallway.

"I need you to get over to my office ASAP," he said.

"Cowboy's out the coma, can it wait?"

"It can't wait, my nigga!" he ended the call abruptly.

As I stepped back into the room, Savon stood over her brother with her eyes wet. She was happy, cheerful, and bonding with her brother. Cowboy had been in the coma for close to a month, and I hated I had to leave, but this thing with Kamar had to be handled.

"I gotta make a run, it will be quick," I said, looking him in the eye.

"Damn, my nigga, we got a lot to talk about," he said.

"I know, so hold that thought. Please, this is really important."

"I guess, just come back," he said, and we embraced each other.

(FLEX)

Earlier that day...

"Y'all want money? I got some keys for you, just let my family live," I said, standing frozen.

The gunmen patted me down, then took the Glock off my waistline. I had a Mac-90 tucked in the couch of my man cave. If only I could get my hands on it and even the playing field. I glanced in Kim's tear-filled eyes and looked at my boys tied up, feeling guilty. I knew the gun would be a mistake, and I would give them whatever to get us out of this mess. It was too risky for me to have a shootout, plus I didn't even know who this man was. All I knew was my family was being held hostage by some foreigners at this point.

"Humor me and get this money you speak of," he said, holding his gun to my son's head.

I led the way to my man cave. All I had was the heroin that I'd robbed Shareef for. I walked slow as I tried to devise a course of action. Nothing came to mind; I had no clue as to why these men were in my home. Robbery didn't seem the motive, though. I rummaged through my closet, pushing clothes to the side, and there sat a stack of boxes with exposed lining on the floor. Under them was my floor safe, inside containing a Glock 40 with a switch. At this point, I had a decision to make. I would either die like a sucker or go out with a blast. The minute they heard the shots fired, my wife would be executed. There was no telling how many gunmen they had lurking, so I shoved the boxes to the side and opened the safe. I pulled the kilos from the safe as the man stood over me with the barrel to my head. I swept the

40 to the side and fished out the remainder of bricks, a total of 9. I was short one that I put in the building. I stood up.

"Is that it?" the henchman asked.

"Yeah, but listen, whatever he's paying you, I can double," I said in a low, persuasive tone.

"Ha, ha, ha, you're a funny guy. Your greed and narcissism is what got you in this position right now," he said in a baritone voice.

He walked me back to where my family was hostage. Calvin was going into an autistic fit as he jerked and squirmed in his chair; the twins sat with a mug on their faces as I looked over at them.

"Everything's going to be okay, boys." I looked to our captor. "You got what you want, now let my family go," I said.

The man began to laugh hysterically. "You're a fool if you think this is what I came for. Do you know who I am?" he said. I wasn't sure if it was a statement or question.

I shook my head and shrugged.

"I am the owner of the kilos in front of us. I count 9, there is one missing. Where is it?" he said while motioning toward the blocks in front of us.

I was dumbfounded by the statement. "I don't understand. What are you saying?"

"My name is Saleen, and I am telling you that you are a traitor, a no-good, conniving snake!" He rose from his seat and circled the table like a shark in bloody water. "You killed someone dear to me, and for the lust of what sits before us . . ." he spoke meticulously, stalking and tormenting each member of my family one by one. When he got to Kim, he ripped the duct tape from her mouth. "Let's see what your wife has to say about your infidelities with my nephew, Shareef," he said.

At the mention of his name, a chill went across my body.

"Fletcher, give them what they want, please," she'd used my government name.

"I . . . I . . . didn't . . . kill him. Shareef was my brother, we . . ." I tried to lie.

"Liar! You are a murderous traitor, but also a businessman, so I will negotiate with you today," he said.

Kim had begun to sob loudly. "Quiet her down," Saleen ordered, and a large man went to her and struck her in the mouth. I tried to lunge at him. *PEW! PEW!*

"AH SHIT!" I yelped in agony as I was hit with a bullet to the arm and leg. I stumbled in front of Saleen as the gunmen sat me back in the chair.

"Now do I have your attention?" he said.

"Uhm, what do we do from here?" I grunted.

"You sold my family for this drug in front of us. This price is a million. I offer you a deal today, I offer you the deity of choice. You want to live or die? Are you ready to do business?" he asked.

"You don't have to do this, take my life."

He chuckled at the remark. "Your death is certain; it is worth less at this point. Another must die. This is what we call blood money in my country. Now make your choice."

Saleen was the spawn of the devil. My wife and I had been married for some time, with everything we wanted. I looked to Calvin, who hadn't a clue of what was going on, but was enraged nonetheless. The twins were fully competent; both had promising futures. One was smart, and the other liked to play basketball. Kim had a promising future. "The clock is ticking. This offer will expire soon."

I dropped my head, a tear slid down my face. "Fuck," I muttered. My head was spinning. I didn't know what to do.

"Make the choice," Saleen said sharply.

"I'm sorry, babe." I nodded in her direction. *Boc!* The shot echoed through the house as Kim's brains splattered the side of Calvin's face as he went into a rageful fit.

"Everything will be okay, I lo—" *BOC! BOC!* My words had been silenced.

(SALEEN)

"Let us go. We have no more business here," I said. My men gathered the drugs and we headed for the door. I looked over my shoulder at the young children and shook my head. "Such a shame. Americans and their greed."

"What should we do about the kids?" my henchman asked.

"Untie them. Their father has determined their future," I said, and we exited the house with the bag of drugs. I reached Kamar's office in 30 minutes. I had some unfinished business with Zaro. My men posted all around the shop as we awaited his arrival. Kamar thought very highly of the young man, and it was a pity that he'd inserted himself into a cutthroat lifestyle. This game I played was at a higher level, and there was no margin for error. Kamar sat at the desk across from me; he and I had a good relationship, and I valued his judgment while respecting his choices. Him bringing Flex into the loop was a bad choice, though, and now Shareef lay dead because of it. I had the weight of the world on my shoulders. I thought back to the day I'd met him.

AFGHANISTAN, 2002...

I hid in the confines of the Afghan mountains with an active warrant for my arrest. I had bombs exploding on the exterior of the mountain as the troops searched for my rabbit hole. Two of my brothers hid out with me as I was on what the United States called a terrorist watch list. I was claimed to have ties to Al-Qaida. Inside the caves, we were hidden with an arsenal of weapons and 2,000 kilos of the purest form of heroin. I was well connected with the Afghans and Iranians and was a supplier of drugs, not terror. The U.S. had their beliefs that the ties I did have were minimal, but I funded their terror program anyway, solely on the basis of security for me and my men to move the heroin safely through Mid-Eastern passages. Suddenly I heard men talking overhead.

"Secure the perimeter . . . CLEAR!" a man's voice shouted. Then came a tumble.

"GRENADE!" I shouted, then ducked for cover. There was a loud explosion followed by the crumbling of rocks. I crawled around the cave floor in darkness as I coughed and gagged on the dirt and debris. I felt the bodies of my comrades as I tried to find safety, but there was nowhere to go. Then I heard footsteps, boots coming toward me. Rocks crunched under his feet as the man got closer, and he stopped to look around. His military M16 scanned the area as he moved about the cave and got closer to me.

"We got 3 dead," he yelled back up to the other troops.

I lay still, trying to play dead, as it was rumored to work on some of the troops. "Hopefully this one," I thought. He stopped at the drugs and started putting them in his vest when suddenly I coughed from sucking in too many debris. He swung his weapon in my direction and flashed the light in my face. I was caught in the headlights.

"Ad Daar . . . you're the one we're looking for. There's a 2-million-dollar price on your head," he said.

I sat and looked at the man with a pleading stare. I would rather die than to go to a U.S. prison. I searched my surrounding area with my eyes, but my AK was under rubble . . . he knew what I was searching for.

"There is no need to fear me. Do you speak English?" he asked.

"I can offer you a chance for great wealth and security with your help. You'll prosper far more than the 2 million your government offers for my capture," I replied. He stepped closer, which meant I had his attention.

"Speak on it," he said, then lowered his rifle.

"Help me fake my death and I have an endless supply of Afghan heroin readily available in the U.S. for you. All you have to do is let your people know that everyone in the cave is dead and there are 2,000 kilos here now for you and your team to split amongst each other. I have a nephew in the U.S. His name is Shareef. He will supply you for further business, and you will have an open line with me . . ." I was about to take a heavy risk by giving him my new identity. I was hiding in the cave until I could change my appearance in Iran . . . "I go by Saleen now." I couldn't see his face clearly in the darkness, but the silence meant I had his attention. Then he responded . . .

"My name is Kamar, and I was forced into this White man's war for oil. I will go see your nephew in a few weeks. I'm about to be kicked out the army. Where is he located?"

"Illinois, the state. Rockford, the city."

"That's where I'm located also."

"Kamar, what's going on down there?" his radio chirped.

"Everybody is dead, including Ad Daar, body parts everywhere," he called back.

"Bring us something to confirm," his superior chirped.

I had to think of something. I huffed, frustrated, then it came to me. I had to take a major risk . . . "You have a knife?"

He pulled from his sidearm; it was rather large and nasty-looking.

"You have to cut my finger off," I said.

I covered my mouth to drown out my yelling. In a quick motion, he was down, and I was a free man . . .

(ZAMAD)

U.S.P. Beaumont...

I walked with my gang to the chow hall as we moved through the first gate to get our meal. I looked over my shoulder, and Red was on my heels. He was sticking to me like glue, almost as if he knew something was about to happen. Popeye had the hit in motion; however, they had to drop him away from me, otherwise, I would be obligated to aid and assist Red. Red and I were leaders in separate organizations; I hated him, but I couldn't let it show. I had a friend from my same city who would take over once Red's death occurred. Then, I would have both gangs at my disposal. It was a power move on my behalf, but most of all, it was the first step toward getting myself out of prison.

Red's security detail stayed in close proximity. When we entered the chow hall, he was stopped by Spider, the head dirty white boy, and then he hung back from me to speak to him. I scanned the area and noticed Popeye's men standing in position. I got a read on their demeanor, and it appeared the hit was about to take place at any moment. Soon after, I heard the C/O yell, "All inmates on the ground!" They dispatched the pepper spray, and everyone started coughing and gagging. I swiveled my head to get a view of what was happening; medical had arrived and immediately started giving the victim chest compressions. That was a good sign. I was sure the victim was Red, and either he was dead or on his way to be dead. I spun back toward my guys, but there was nothing left to see, and all that could be heard was chatter over what had happened. A lot of them were claiming him to be dead, but nothing was for sure. I hoped this was it.

Two days later...

I sat at the desk in my cell, my roommate lay on the top bunk. The prison had gone on lock-down due to Red's murder. Popeye had sent some dumb white boy Spanish kid to do the job; turns out, he had just gotten to the prison and wanted to run Surreno. They utilized him as a weapon, the color of his skin helping him get into places they couldn't. Plus, he had nothing to lose, as he was serving out four life sentences. His initiation into the gang had him pose as a white boy in order to divert attention from any Mexican. The whites controlled the minority inside, and they would have to take the blame for the hit. The white boy who'd done it would spend the next 10 years in an ADX, where the worst of the worst are housed. He was easily disposable, as most overly eager men in prison were. In the U.S.P., you were either a wolf or a sheep.

"That's fucked up what happened with Red," Capo said as he got off his bed.

"I know, but sacrifices needed to be made," I replied with a devilish grin.

He looked at me curiously, like he was trying to decode the message. I nodded slowly, not saying a word. His mouth dropped. "You baked that cake?" he asked. "Wait, don't answer that."

I smiled then rolled up some Kush. I took a deep pull, exhaled, then passed the joint. We sat and smoked for a while. Then I decided to break out the phone and make a call to Popeye's people. The fentanyl blues were a go, and I needed someone to pick them up. I could put Kamar in the mix of this particular plan, as everyone has a part to play. I would inject him when the time called for it though. I dialed my nigga Frank from Memphis Mob; we'd done time together, and he had just got out and was looking for a come-up. He would be the right candidate for the job.

The puzzle I was putting together was coming along perfectly. This was an exit to a life bid. After I finished making my calls, I asked Capo if he wanted to make some calls before I put it away. He called someone in Washington, and turns out he had some hitters out there from Hollystreet Hellraiser Crip, judging by how he spoke to the person on the phone. For the rest of the night, I picked his brain on who he was and where he was headed; turns out we had the same thing in common. We both wanted our freedom and money. Capo had promised his shooters would look after my son. Zaro would need the aid of some new soldiers with Flex out the picture. Calico would lay in wait until Thunder and Kato got released, and they would wreak havoc on the streets. Kamar, Flex, Thunder, Calico, and myself all ran together before I came to prison. That was until Flex crossed me; it was good then, and I kept the thought, "Nothing beats a cross like a double cross." I relaxed, back in deep thought.

"Big homie, you a smart nigga for what you doing," Capo said.

"They gone see me again, and bow down to the greatest," I replied.

"I just want to see my lil' niggas eating. Hopefully, ya son will accept them like family. My folks is loyal, fam. They gone die for ya son if he feed them healthy meals."

"I'ma make sure shit good, my nigga. Sit back and enjoy the ride. We got a lot to do in the morning," I said and closed my eyes.

(ZARO)

Zoo and I drove to the auto lot; I had Zoo tag along because Kamar sounded shaky over the phone. Kamar was a calculated old head, and I didn't want to walk into a trap. Nylon, Bang, and Telay trailed me in a Striker as extra support. We all had Glocks and switches, and between the two vehicles, there was at least 500 rounds of Hydroshock. Telay Neem held my back in case shit went sideways. I didn't know what to expect from Kamar; old niggas thought of the game like chess, and I had to stay a move ahead of him. I thought about what he could possibly want over and over in my head, but nothing came up. I got a cloud. He'd surprised me with that crazy Muslim-looking guy earlier, and now the same niggas were back at the lot after killing off every nigga in Waaco. I was trying to make sure I wouldn't be next. On the other hand, if I don't show up, it could make me appear guilty or scared, and I was neither of those. News about Waaco had buzzed Facebook and Instagram. I'd recognized the *terrorists*, as they were called on most media platforms. Witnesses recounted how they shot up the projects with skill, and the terrorists' bow-ties were familiar.

I knew they were the same men I'd met at the car lot. The Muslim men took the city's murder rate up in one day.

I turned into the lot and slid the car in park, noticing the same Tahoe's were out front. I looked over at Zoo; he held his Gen 5 with the switch and two sticks.

"Be ready for anything. If shit looks fucked up, squeeze till yo' shit empty," I said coldly.

He hacked the slide on his glizzy, as I did the same and patted my vest, ensuring my shit was tight. The Muslims stood erect with faces like stone as we slid out of the Magnum in unison. The night's air was frigid, the atmosphere filled with death's aroma; its lustful taste sent a chill down my spine as I tucked my gun in my waistband. Zoo and I made our way towards the lobby as the men mugged us as we walked past. They didn't try to hide their weapons, compact Uzi's, and my heart knocked hard. I couldn't let them see me sweat, but Zoo looked around unfazed. I was glad to have him by my side; he was ready for whatever. When we got inside, the men drew their weapons, and we froze in our tracks. I thought to myself, "This would be the shoot-out of the century," and I looked back to see Telay ready to react.

To Be Continued...

Lock Down Publications and Ca$h Presents
Assisted Publishing Packages

Due to an increase in the price of services we have increased our prices. The prices below reflect the price increase as of 11/1/24.

BASIC PACKAGE	UPGRADED PACKAGE
$699	**$1000**
Editing	Typing
Cover Design	Editing
Formatting	Cover Design
	Formatting
	Upload eBooks to Amazon
	Upload Paperback to Amazon
ADVANCE PACKAGE	**LDP SUPREME PACKAGE**
$1,400	**$1,700**
Typing	Typing
Editing (line editing/content)	Editing (line editing/content)
Cover Design	Cover Design
Formatting	Formatting
Copyright Registration	Copyright Registration
Proofreading	Proofreading
Upload eBooks to Amazon	Set up Amazon Account
Upload Paperback to Amazon	Upload eBooks to Amazon
	Upload Paperback to Amazon
	Advertise on LDP's Amazon and Facebook Page

***

Other services available upon request.
Additional charges may apply

Lock Down Publications
P.O. Box 944
Stockbridge, GA 30281-9998
Phone: 470 303-9761
Email: lockdownpublications@gmail.com

141

Submission Guideline

Submit the first three chapters of your completed manuscript to ldpsubmissions@gmail.com. In the subject line add **Your Book's Title**. The manuscript must be in a Word Doc file and sent as an attachment. Document should be in Times New Roman, double spaced, and in size 12 font. Also, provide your synopsis and full contact information. If sending multiple submissions, they must each be in a separate email.

Have a story but no way to send it electronically? You can still submit to LDP/Ca$h Presents. Send in the first three chapters, written or typed, of your completed manuscript to:

LDP: Submissions Dept
P.O. Box 944
Stockbridge, GA 30281-9998

DO NOT send original manuscript. Must be a duplicate. Provide your synopsis and a cover letter containing your full contact information.

Thanks for considering LDP and Ca$h Presents.

NEW RELEASES

BLOODLINE OF A SAVAGE 1-3
THESE VICIOUS STREETS 1-3
RELENTLESS GOON 1-3
BY PRINCE A. TAUHID

THE BUTTERFLY MAFIA 1-3
BY FUMIYA PAYNE

A THUG'S STREET PRINCESS 1&2
BY MEESHA

CITY OF SMOKE 3
BY MOLOTTI

GET IT IN SLUGS 1 &2
BY B. STALL

STANDING ON HER BUSINESS 1&2
BY DG SANTANA

STEPPERS 1,2&3
THE REAL BADDIES OF CHI-RAQ
BY KING RIO

THE LANE 1&2
BY KEN-KEN SPENCE

THUG OF SPADES 1&2
LOVE IN THE TRENCHES 2
CORNER BOYS
BY COREY ROBINSON

TIL DEATH 3
BY ARYANNA

DRILL CITY | ZAY'TOWVEN

THE BIRTH OF A GANGSTER 4
BY DELMONT PLAYER

PRODUCT OF THE STREETS 1-3
BY DEMOND "MONEY" ANDERSON

NO TIME FOR ERROR
BY KEESE

MONEY HUNGRY DEMONS 1-2
BY TRANAY ADAMS

HUB CITY MENACE 1-3
BY J. WHITE

A THUGGISH PASSION 1&2
LAND OF DA HOOLIGANZ 1-4
KILLAZ ON STANDBY 1&2
BY IRA B.

FO'EVA ROLLIN 1&2
BY ASSA RAYMOND BAKER

THE LEVEL UP 1&3
BY LUXURY KING

Coming Soon from Lock Down Publications/Ca$h Presents

IF YOU CROSS ME ONCE 6
ANGEL V
By Anthony Fields

A THUGS STREET PRINCESS 3
By Meesha

CORNER BOYS 2
By Corey Robinson

THA TAKEOVER
By Keith Chandler

BETRAYAL OF A G 2
By Ray Vinci

SAVAGE FAMILY EMPIRE 1&2
SOULLESS GOON 1,2&3
THE DIRTY SIDE OF MONEY 1,2&3
By Prince

FOR MY ENEMY'S SAKE
AMBITIONS OF A SLIDER
FRESH OFF DA PORCH
By IRA B.

BY THE TRUCKLOAD 1-4
TIPPIN' THE SCALES 1-3
BAD BITCHES WIT GUNZ 3
PROBLEM SOLVED 2
By Christopher "Diesel" Hornezes

Available Now

RESTRAINING ORDER 1 & 2
By **CA$H & Coffee**

LOVE KNOWS NO BOUNDARIES 1-3
By **Coffee**

RAISED AS A GOON I, II, III & IV
BRED BY THE SLUMS I, II, III
BLAST FOR ME I & II
ROTTEN TO THE CORE I II III
A BRONX TALE I, II, III
DUFFLE BAG CARTEL I II III IV V VI
HEARTLESS GOON I II III IV V
A SAVAGE DOPEBOY I II
DRUG LORDS I II III
CUTTHROAT MAFIA I II
KING OF THE TRENCHES
By **Ghost**

LAY IT DOWN I & II
LAST OF A DYING BREED I II
BLOOD STAINS OF A SHOTTA I & II III
By **Jamaica**

LOYAL TO THE GAME I II III
LIFE OF SIN I, II III
By **TJ & Jelissa**

IF LOVING HIM IS WRONG…I & II
LOVE ME EVEN WHEN IT HURTS I II III
By **Jelissa**

PUSH IT TO THE LIMIT
By **Bre' Hayes**

DRILL CITY | ZAY'TOWVEN

BLOODY COMMAS I & II
SKI MASK CARTEL I, II & III
KING OF NEW YORK I II, III IV V
RISE TO POWER I II III
COKE KINGS I II III IV V
BORN HEARTLESS I II III IV
KING OF THE TRAP I II
By **T.J. Edwards**

WHEN THE STREETS CLAP BACK I & II III
THE HEART OF A SAVAGE I II III IV
MONEY MAFIA I II
LOYAL TO THE SOIL I II III
By **Jibril Williams**

A DISTINGUISHED THUG STOLE MY HEART I II & III
LOVE SHOULDN'T HURT I II III IV
RENEGADE BOYS 1-4
PAID IN KARMA 1-3
SAVAGE STORMS 1-3
AN UNFORESEEN LOVE 1-3
BABY, I'M WINTERTIME COLD 1-3
A THUG'S STREET PRINCESS 1&2
By **Meesha**

A GANGSTER'S CODE 1-3
A GANGSTER'S SYN 1-3
THE SAVAGE LIFE 1-3
CHAINED TO THE STREETS 1-3
BLOOD ON THE MONEY 1-3
A GANGSTA'S PAIN 1-3
BEAUTIFUL LIES AND UGLY TRUTHS
CHURCH IN THESE STREETS
By **J-Blunt**

CUM FOR ME 1-8
An LDP Erotica Collaboration

147

DRILL CITY | ZAY'TOWVEN

BLOOD OF A BOSS 1-5
SHADOWS OF THE GAME
TRAP BASTARD
By **Askari**

THE STREETS BLEED MURDER 1-3
THE HEART OF A GANGSTA 1-3
By **Jerry Jackson**

WHEN A GOOD GIRL GOES BAD
By **Adrienne**

THE COST OF LOYALTY 1-3
By **Kweli**

BRIDE OF A HUSTLA 1-3
THE FETTI GIRLS 1-3
CORRUPTED BY A GANGSTA 1-4
BLINDED BY HIS LOVE
THE PRICE YOU PAY FOR LOVE 1-3
DOPE GIRL MAGIC 1-3
By **Destiny Skai**

A KINGPIN'S AMBITION
A KINGPIN'S AMBITION II
I MURDER FOR THE DOUGH
By **Ambitious**

TRUE SAVAGE 1-7
DOPE BOY MAGIC 1-3
MIDNIGHT CARTEL 1-3
CITY OF KINGZ 1&2
NIGHTMARE ON SILENT AVE
THE PLUG OF LIL MEXICO 1&2
CLASSIC CITY
By **Chris Green**

DRILL CITY | ZAY'TOWVEN

A GANGSTER'S REVENGE 1-4
THE BOSS MAN'S DAUGHTERS 1-5
A SAVAGE LOVE 1&2
BAE BELONGS TO ME 1&2
A HUSTLER'S DECEIT 1-3
WHAT BAD BITCHES DO 1-3
SOUL OF A MONSTER 1-3
KILL ZONE
A DOPE BOY'S QUEEN 1-3
TIL DEATH 1-3
IMMA DIE BOUT MINE 1-6
DYING FOR LIKES
By **Aryanna**

A DOPEBOY'S PRAYER
By **Eddie "Wolf" Lee**

THE KING CARTEL 1-3
By **Frank Gresham**

THESE NIGGAS AIN'T LOYAL 1-3
By **Nikki Tee**

GANGSTA SHYT 1-3
By **CATO**

THE ULTIMATE BETRAYAL
By **Phoenix**

BOSS'N UP 1-3
By **Royal Nicole**

I LOVE YOU TO DEATH
By **Destiny J**

I RIDE FOR MY HITTA
I STILL RIDE FOR MY HITTA
By **Misty Holt**

DRILL CITY | ZAY'TOWVEN

LOVE & CHASIN' PAPER
By **Qay Crockett**

TO DIE IN VAIN
SINS OF A HUSTLA
By **ASAD**

BROOKLYN HUSTLAZ
By **Boogsy Morina**

BROOKLYN ON LOCK 1 & 2
By **Sonovia**

GANGSTA CITY
By **Teddy Duke**

A DRUG KING AND HIS DIAMOND 1-3
A DOPEMAN'S RICHES
HER MAN, MINE'S TOO 1&2
CASH MONEY HO'S
THE WIFEY I USED TO BE 1&2
PRETTY GIRLS DO NASTY THINGS
By **Nicole Goosby**

LIPSTICK KILLAH 1-3
CRIME OF PASSION 1-3
FRIEND OR FOE 1-3
By **Mimi**

TRAPHOUSE KING 1-3
KINGPIN KILLAZ 1-3
STREET KINGS 1&2
PAID IN BLOOD 1&2
CARTEL KILLAZ 1-3
DOPE GODS 1&2
By **Hood Rich**

THE STREETS ARE CALLING
By **Duquie Wilson**

DRILL CITY | ZAY'TOWVEN

STEADY MOBBN' 1-3
THE STREETS STAINED MY SOUL 1-3
By **Marcellus Allen**

WHO SHOT YA 1-3
SON OF A DOPE FIEND 1-4
HEAVEN GOT A GHETTO 1&2
SKI MASK MONEY 1&2
By **Renta**

GORILLAZ IN THE BAY 1-4
TEARS OF A GANGSTA 1/&2
3X KRAZY 1&2
STRAIGHT BEAST MODE 1&2
By **DE'KARI**

TRIGGADALE 1-3
MURDA WAS THE CASE 1-3
By **Elijah R. Freeman**

SLAUGHTER GANG 1-3
RUTHLESS HEART 1-3
By **Willie Slaughter**

GOD BLESS THE TRAPPERS 1-3
THESE SCANDALOUS STREETS 1-3
FEAR MY GANGSTA 1-5
THESE STREETS DON'T LOVE NOBODY 1-2
BURY ME A G 1-5
A GANGSTA'S EMPIRE 1-4
THE DOPEMAN'S BODYGAURD 1&2
THE REALEST KILLAZ 1-3
THE LAST OF THE OGS 1-3
By **Tranay Adams**

MARRIED TO A BOSS 1-3
By **Destiny Skai & Chris Green**

KINGZ OF THE GAME 1-7
CRIME BOSS 1-4
By **Playa Ray**

FUK SHYT
By **Blakk Diamond**

DON'T F#CK WITH MY HEART 1&2
By **Linnea**

ADDICTED TO THE DRAMA 1-3
IN THE ARM OF HIS BOSS
By **Jamila**

LOYALTY AIN'T PROMISED 1&2
By **Keith Williams**

YAYO 1-4
A SHOOTER'S AMBITION 1&2
BRED IN THE GAME
By **S. Allen**

TRAP GOD 1-3
RICH $AVAGE 1-3
MONEY IN THE GRAVE 1-3
CARTEL MONEY 1&2
By **Martell Troublesome Bolden**

FOREVER GANGSTA 1&2
GLOCKS ON SATIN SHEETS 1&2
By **Adrian Dulan**

TOE TAGZ 1-4
LEVELS TO THIS SHYT 1&2
IT'S JUST ME AND YOU
By **Ah'Million**

DRILL CITY | ZAY'TOWVEN

KINGPIN DREAMS 1-3
RAN OFF ON DA PLUG
By **Paper Boi Rari**

THE STREETS MADE ME 1-3
By **Larry D. Wright**

CONFESSIONS OF A GANGSTA 1-4
CONFESSIONS OF A JACKBOY 1-3
CONFESSIONS OF A HITMAN
CONFESSIONS OF A DOPE BOY
By **Nicholas Lock**

I'M NOTHING WITHOUT HIS LOVE
SINS OF A THUG
TO THE THUG I LOVED BEFORE
A GANGSTA SAVED XMAS
IN A HUSTLER I TRUST
By **Monet Dragun**

QUIET MONEY 1-3
THUG LIFE 1-3
EXTENDED CLIP 1&2
A GANGSTA'S PARADISE
By **Trai'Quan**

CAUGHT UP IN THE LIFE 1-3
THE STREETS NEVER LET GO 1-3
By **Robert Baptiste**

NEW TO THE GAME 1-3
MONEY, MURDER & MEMORIES 1-3
By **Malik D. Rice**

CREAM 2-3
THE STREETS WILL TALK
By **Yolanda Moore**

THE STREETS WILL NEVER CLOSE 1-3
By **K'ajji**

LIFE OF A SAVAGE 1-4
A GANGSTA'S QUR'AN 1-4
MURDA SEASON 1-3
GANGLAND CARTEL 1-3
CHI'RAQ GANGSTAS 1-4
KILLERS ON ELM STREET 1-3
JACK BOYZ N DA BRONX 1-3
A DOPEBOY'S DREAM 1-3
JACK BOYS VS DOPE BOYS 1-3
COKE GIRLZ
COKE BOYS
SOSA GANG 1&2
BRONX SAVAGES
BODYMORE KINGPINS
BLOOD OF A GOON
By **Romell Tukes**

CONCRETE KILLA 1-3
VICIOUS LOYALTY 1-3
BLOODY MONEY BAGS
By **Kingpen**

THE ULTIMATE SACRIFICE 1-6
KHADIFI
IF YOU CROSS ME ONCE 1-3
ANGEL 1-4
IN THE BLINK OF AN EYE
By **Anthony Fields**

THE LIFE OF A HOOD STAR
By **Ca$h & Rashia Wilson**

NIGHTMARES OF A HUSTLA 1-3
BLOOD AND GAMES 1&2
By **King Dream**

GHOST MOB
By **Stilloan Robinson**

HARD AND RUTHLESS 1&2
MOB TOWN 251
THE BILLIONAIRE BENTLEYS 1-3
REAL G'S MOVE IN SILENCE
By **Von Diesel**

MOB TIES 1-7
SOUL OF A HUSTLER, HEART OF A KILLER 1-3
GORILLAZ IN THE TRENCHES
OOPS CRY TOO 1&2
THE DAUGHTER OF A CARTEL BOSS
By **SayNoMore**

BODYMORE MURDERLAND 1-3
THE BIRTH OF A GANGSTER 1-4
By **Delmont Player**

FOR THE LOVE OF A BOSS 1&2
By **C. D. Blue**

KILLA KOUNTY 1-5
TENDER
By **Khufu**

MOBBED UP 1-4
THE BRICK MAN 1-5
THE COCAINE PRINCESS 1-10
STEPPERS 1-3
SUPER GREMLIN 1-4
A GANGSTA'S SON
By **King Rio**

MONEY GAME 1&2
By **Smoove Dolla**

DRILL CITY | ZAY'TOWVEN

A GANGSTA'S KARMA 1-5
By **FLAME**

KING OF THE TRENCHES 1-3
By **GHOST & TRANAY ADAMS**

BAD BITCHES WIT GUNZ 1&2
PROBLEM SOLVED
By **"Christopher Diesel" Hornezes**

QUEEN OF THE ZOO 1&2
By **Black Migo**

GRIMEY WAYS 1-3
BETRAYAL OF A G
By **Ray Vinci**

XMAS WITH AN ATL SHOOTER
By **Ca$h & Destiny Skai**

KING KILLA 1&2
By **Vincent "Vitto" Holloway**

BETRAYAL OF A THUG 1&2
By **Fre$h**

COUNTDOWN OF A KILLA 1&2
SEX, MURDER AND GOD 1&2
GUNS DOWN, BOTTOMS UP 1&2
By Lo-Life

THE MURDER QUEENS 1-7
By **Michael Gallon**

FOR THE LOVE OF BLOOD 1-4
By **Jamel Mitchell**

DRILL CITY | ZAY'TOWVEN

HOOD CONSIGLIERE 1&2
NO TIME FOR ERROR
By **Keese**

PROTÉGÉ OF A LEGEND 1,2&3
LOVE IN THE TRENCHES 1&2
By **Corey Robinson**

THE PLUG'S RUTHLESS DAUGHTER 1&2
By **Tony Daniels**

BORN IN THE GRAVE 1-3
CRIME PAYS
By **Self Made Tay**

MOAN IN MY MOUTH
By **XTASY**

TORN BETWEEN A GANGSTER AND A GENTLEMAN
By **J-BLUNT & Miss Kim**

LOYALTY IS EVERYTHING 1-3
CITY OF SMOKE 1-3
By **Molotti**

HERE TODAY GONE TOMORROW 1&2
By **Fly Rock**

WOMEN LIE MEN LIE 1-4
FIFTY SHADES OF SNOW 1-3
STACK BEFORE YOU SPLURGE
GIRLS FALL LIKE DOMINOES
NAÏVE TO THE STREETS
By **ROY MILLIGAN**

PILLOW PRINCESS
By **S. Hawkins**

DRILL CITY | ZAY'TOWVEN

THE BUTTERFLY MAFIA 1-3
SALUTE MY SAVAGERY 1&2
By **Fumiya Payne**

THE LANE 1&2
By Ken-Ken Spence

THE PUSSY TRAP 1-5
By **Nene Capri**

DIRTY DNA
By **Blaque**

SANCTIFIED AND HORNY
by **XTASY**

BOOKS BY LDP'S CEO, CA$H

TRUST IN NO MAN
TRUST IN NO MAN 2
TRUST IN NO MAN 3
BONDED BY BLOOD
SHORTY GOT A THUG
THUGS CRY
THUGS CRY 2
THUGS CRY 3
TRUST NO BITCH
TRUST NO BITCH 2
TRUST NO BITCH 3
TIL MY CASKET DROPS
RESTRAINING ORDER
RESTRAINING ORDER 2
IN LOVE WITH A CONVICT
LIFE OF A HOOD STAR
XMAS WITH AN ATL SHOOTER